THE SOLSTICE GIFT
Behrouz and Lucky on the Longest Night

Avery Cassell

Greenfield, Massachusetts

2019

The Solstice Gift: Behrouz and Lucky on the Longest Night
Copyright ©2019 by Avery Cassell

All rights reserved. No part of this publication may be reproduced, distributed, or transmitted in any form or by any means, including photocopying, recording, or other electronic or mechanical methods, without the prior written permission of the publisher, except in the case of brief quotations embodied in critical reviews and certain other noncommercial uses permitted by copyright law. For permission requests, write to the publisher at the address below.

Stoic Press
averystoicpress@gmail.com
PO Box 766
Greenfield, MA 01301
stoicpress.bigcartel.com

Publisher's Cataloging-in-Publication Data
The solstice gift : Behrouz and Lucky on the longest night/
by Avery Cassell.
First trade paperback original edition.
LCCN 2019919242
ISBN 978-0-578-61622-3
1. Lesbians--Fiction. 2. Sexual minorities--Fiction. 3. Middle-aged persons--Fiction. 4. Bondage (Sexual behavior)--Fiction. 5. Sexual dominance and submission--Fiction. 6. Northampton (Mass.)--Fiction.
PS3603.A86836 S65 2019

This is a work of fiction. All characters and incidents are products of the author's overactive imagination. Any resemblance to actual persons, living or dead, is purely coincidental. Portions of this book are nonfiction. Certain places, events, and identifying characteristics have been changed.

Copy editor and book designer: Diane Kanzler of Stoic Press
Stoic Press logo designed by Diane Kanzler of Stoic Press
Cover photograph by Diane Kanzler of Stoic Press

Second printing 2023

CHAPTERS

	Page
Prologue	5
One: The Solstice Gift	9
Two: "You Don't Need to Get Me Anything. I Have Everything I Could Possibly Want."	11
Three: Dant y Llew Helps Out	19
Four: Pooh Bear and the Longest Night, Performing the Sexual Narrative with Three Bodies	23
Five: Honey Campbell of Ye Olde Pull My Daisy Shoppe	27
Six: Honey Quotes Emma Goldman at the Orphans Harvest Potluck Dinner	31
Seven: Penny Posy and the Frisky Bunny Diorama	35
Eight: Leroy King and the Triple Daddies	39
Nine: Marilyn Shoemaker and the Five Colleges	45
Ten: The Solstice Gift Choices	61
Eleven: An Unseasonably Warm Night	65
Twelve: A Showdown at the Co-Op	69
Thirteen: Butter Chicken and a Winner	83
Fourteen: Pearl Harbor Day by Paradise Pond	85
Fifteen: Lucky Gives Behrouz a Surprise Holiday Gift	87
Sixteen: Service is as Service Does	93
Recipe: *Ghormeh Sabzi*	99

*This book is dedicated to strong, stubborn,
and stoic women everywhere.*

PROLOGUE

Lucky and I moved to western Massachusetts in 2019. Before we left San Francisco, we heard rumors about Northampton and the Pioneer Valley, sexy stories that we hoped were true but that we doubted. You may have heard the stories too. Dykes and queers throughout the northeast whispered tales of lesbian debauchery. The naughty tales circulated over lattes in cafes, over cocktails in gay bars, over hummus during potlucks and, more recently, while carrying signs and demonstrating against the government.

We chalked it up to general lesbian sexual shenanigans—you know the kind. When I moved to San Francisco way back in the 1980s, my neighbors were a middle-aged gay bear couple, both leather-clad, bearded, and chunky. The first night in my new apartment, Abe and Kevin knocked on my door, bearing a little Fiestaware dish of fresh strawberries as a welcome-to-the-building gift. We became pals, often ate dinner together, and ran to and fro between our apartments. One night while we shared a curried Indian pizza and watched the latest season of Downton Abby, Abe confessed that dyke sex frightened him. I was astonished; this burly, pierced leather god was scared by dykes fucking? Well, it turned out that Abe and Kevin had recently gone to a bear weekend retreat at Russian River that coincided with a dyke drumming retreat, and the town was flooded with horny, cruising dykes and bears. Wide-eyed with amazement, Abe told me that he and Kevin were kept up all night long by the cacophony of dykes fucking. Abe nudged my leg, winked, and slyly said, "They never stopped! How on earth do you girls do it?" I just blushed in response.

More recently on one cool and foggy San Francisco night, while bonding over peanut tofu satay curry, our friend Poppy swore that her young cousin—who was studying at Smith College and majoring in Medieval Studies—had actually been picked as the Solstice Gift last December! That certainly set our wheels spinning. What if this urban legend was true? This was truly something that I could imagine Lucky and I doing, and the icing on the cupcake was that the instigators of this mythological annual romp were also an older butch couple… just like us.

When we got ready to abandon San Francisco, the Northampton area became a possibility. We heard positive things about the Pioneer Valley: there was a large dyke and queer community, it was liberal, and the arts were respected and encouraged. There was the Pie Bar in Florence, a mirror image of Mission Pie in the Mission. We heard that there was a regular butch meet-up in the area, similar to the Bulldaggers group in Oakland. Pull My Daisy Floral Shoppe was known for their artsy arrangements that drew gawking fans every time they changed out their window display, much like IXIA in the Castro. Ebony spoke highly of Northampton; her second cousin Raven had moved there last year and started a queer open mic. If we moved to the Pioneer Valley, would we meet this legendary butch-on-butch couple? We wondered what they were like—perhaps they were just an alternative reality version of us. A dreamy reinvention, as it were, much like Dorothy and her friends in the Land of Oz.

Love,

Behrooz   Lucky

PART ONE: THE PAST

CHAPTER ONE
The Solstice Gift

I'm Behrouz, and my wife is Lucky. At first, I couldn't decide what to call our tradition: choosing the potential gifts, posting their names on the tree by Paradise Pond, pondering and processing, the final decision, and the lascivious end result. I mean, neither of us are exactly Christians and we don't really celebrate Christmas. We don't go to Christmas Eve mass or open a chocolate advent calendar during December, although we do bake cookies, trim a tree, hang stockings, and recreate and age Aunt Flo's fruitcake each year. Hell, we don't even celebrate Yule like all good witches do, welcoming the longest night of the year with burning the Yule log and dancing around bonfires, although perhaps we should. When I jokingly called it our Festivus gift, Lucky teased me and said that it was only Festivus on *Seinfeld*, a television sitcom show. What do I know; I've never seen *Seinfeld*. Not even once. What I **do** know is that we have our own tradition each winter solstice on December 21st, and the ritual takes longer to prepare for than Aunt Flo's admittedly scrumptious rum-soaked cake. Lucky and I finally settled on calling it the Solstice Gift.

We eagerly start our list of possible gifts in the end of June on the summer solstice, and we write them down in our purple moleskin Solstice Gift ledger. It's like going through the Sears catalog for Christmas toys and making up our wishes for

Santa, but with much more adult desires: brilliant wit and plump lips instead of Candyland and pogo sticks. We narrow it down to three or so then publicly announce the list of gift contenders in the end of September on the autumnal equinox. We choose the winner over breakfast on the first Sunday of December. On Pearl Harbor Day we send them an engraved invitation to our winter solstice celebration, and we unwrap our gift after supper on the night of the winter solstice.

When we created our winter solstice tradition, we were newly married and as horny as only two erudite, kinky, older butches could be. You know the type—we'd been around the block so many times that we had road maps and shortcuts in our respective brains and bloodstreams. It all started because of that saying that older folks piously intone when asked what they'd like for Christmas or their birthday: "You don't need to get me anything. I have everything I could possibly want." It always makes me roll my eyes and want to buy them something outlandish like a sleepy baby camel or a velvet painting of the Mona Lisa to go over the sofa.

CHAPTER TWO
"You Don't Need to Get Me Anything. I Have Everything I Could Possibly Want."

November 2013

One night in November after a particularly fine dinner of gingered salmon and cauliflower gratin with cock sucking for dessert, I asked the lovely Lucky what she wanted for Christmas. We snuggled beneath a thick comforter in a peaceful postcoital haze, and the cats had finally decided it was safe to venture back on the bed. When I asked Lucky what she wanted for Christmas, she kissed my forehead and murmured, "You don't need to get me anything, baby. I have everything I could possibly want."

I squirmed against her chest, rolled my eyes, and said, "Really, silly goose? Everything you could possibly want? Just fifteen minutes ago you were begging me to suck your clit and fuck your ass at the same time, but I couldn't be in both places at once. Wouldn't you like to have your clit sucked and your ass fucked concurrently, sweetpea?" I tweaked her nipple. She moaned and shoved her thigh between my legs. I wiggled to get closer, opened my legs to smoosh my cunt against Lucky's thigh, and coated her leg with a pool of hot, sticky come.

Lucky moaned again. My mental gears were turning. What if we really could figure out a way to be in more than one place at once, grow another couple of hands, fuck asses and cunts while diddling clits and cocks? "I have an idea," I said as I drew the comforter up to my chin. "I think we should have a Solstice Gift. It would be a little something that we give to one another and that we share. For fun. And we could do it every year!" I giggled deviously.

"Eh? What did you have in mind?" Lucky asked sleepily as she nibbled my salty shoulder.

"Let's have a threesome every winter solstice, kind of like pagan sex magic circles…do those even exist anymore, for real? Anyway, we could pick a dyke each year and make a ritual of it. It would be loads of fun!"

"A threesome? Hey, threesomes used to be my specialty in college! Hell, I studied biology and threesomes at Berkeley. Did I ever tell you about how I got my name?" I could sense Lucky's growing interest in my scheme.

"What, because you got lucky so often?" I smirked.

"Ummm, kind of. My mom named me Pierrette. She had a thing for the old-fashioned French mimes. The female ones were called Pierrette and the male ones were named Pierrot. They were romantic buffoons wearing huge ruff collars, white clothing, and sometimes black and white striped tights. When I was thirteen, I came out as a baby butch and decided to change my name."

"As adolescents do," I murmured.

"I wanted something boyish but also something more normal. I was tired of having such a weird name. Pierrette was a lot to live up to in the cul-de-sacs of Midwestern Ohio. I didn't want to stray too far, though, and decided upon Pierre. My mom, Betty, was livid. She and I continued to fight over femininity until I moved out, and she and Dad divorced," Lucky continued.

"So why aren't you Pierre? Did you do that thing where you changed your name every few months? My daughter Theo did that, and it just about drove me to pieces. There was a period between thirteen and seventeen when I never knew from day-to-day who would greet me in the morning! Theo, Jackie, TJ, Zoe, and Jack are just the names I remember off the top of my head," I reminisced.

"Nooooo." Lucky looked chagrined. "Remember, I said that I had a thing for threesomes? I became known on campus for my…." Lucky looked thoughtful. "Well, for my skill in arranging threesomes with the unlikeliest combinations of women. Sorority girls, jocks, activists, beauty queens, cheerleaders, librarians, hippies, punks…I had a wide range and I loved them all."

I chuckled, thinking of Lucky as a young butch Lothario fucking her way through Berkeley's oak-lined campus.

"Those were good times. I remember once I managed to get a lesbian separatist and a sorority girl together. Gina was the sweetest southern Georgia peach dyke, short and juicy with one of those no-holds-barred Dorothy Hamill haircuts that all the dykes in the 1970s had, and Kendra was a straight girl from Harlem, tall and skinny, with enormous dark brown eyes, cornrows, and a sexy overbite." Lucky's eyes took on a dreamy look at the memories.

"This is fabulous! Did this just happen magically? Like, did you have a fiery moment in the library while studying together, your eyes meeting over notes and physics textbooks, then fleeing to frantically fuck in a nearby dorm?" I asked.

"I'll tell you my secrets to a great three way." Lucky straightened up in bed and explained her threesome rules helpfully and seriously. "First, there needs to be a general mutual agreement on what's hot. People with strong fetishes who only get off in conjunction with that fetish don't usually work in a group setting unless that fetish is what draws you together. If you've got to get pissed on to come and the other two are not into watersports, it's a no-go. Second, you know how a successful dinner party is a conglomeration of people? In a memorable party, you want people with enough differences so that they are intriguing to each other. You want painters next to lawyers, next to vet techs, next to philosophy professors, and so on. It's the same idea for an exceptional three way but even more so. That patina of exotic difference adds to the feeling of sexual transgression which, in turn, ramps up the excitement. If they run in different social circles that's even better. This means that it's unlikely to have embarrassing gossip about being slutty bite them in the ass later. So, a lesbian separatist, a sorority girl, and yours truly was pure threesome gold."

"Wow, you really thought this through!" I was impressed by Lucky's dedication to the pursuit of pleasure.

"I liked to fuck, and I liked to make girls come," Lucky said modestly. "As Napoleon Dynamite said, 'Girls only like guys who have great skills,' and I had skills, like kissing skills, fucking skills, seduction skills."

"Sometimes you're such 13-year-old boy!" I snorted. "So, threesomes were the most expedient ways of spreading the love, sprinkling orgasms all over the Berkeley Hills like a dyke Tinkerbell sprinkling pixie dust?" I snuggled next to Lucky, resting my head on her soft left breast.

"But without the wings. Your idea, though, I think we could make it work. But we're older nowadays, not quite as agile…" Lucky trailed off as she contemplated logistics.

"We have infinitely more experience, practice, and sexual self-awareness now. Our knees may be creaky, but our loins are willing!" I exclaimed excitedly, feeling like a mountain climber planting their flag on the rocky peak and proclaiming "Excelsior!" I started to plan our winter threesome in my head. This was a hell of lot more thrilling than planning our annual Orphans Harvest Potluck Dinner.

"We could have rules!" I blurted. Lucky and I like rules; after all, she's a copy editor and I'm a retired librarian. Organization fills us with glee, and weekends are incomplete without at least one to-do list. I loved diagramming sentences as a young girl, fitting each word into its proper place, marveling at syntax and structure. Spreadsheets and charts started racing through my mind.

"Rules? Like what kind of rules? Are we talking about time limits or activity guidelines?" Lucky asked with a degree of skepticism. "I'm not so sure about this…I mean, the whole idea here is to have fun!"

"Bear with me, baby. Here are the rules. First off, no repeats—dykes are only chosen once. They stay the entire night for maximum fuck gratification." I felt myself segue into organizational mode, my inner librarian gleefully planning our threesome fucking guidelines.

"Hmmm. If they stay the night, then we should have a traditional fancy morning-after breakfast before they go back home. You know how we always have chicken sausage and waffles with blackberry compote on Christmas morning? Maybe we could make a little breakfast casserole!" Lucky tweaked my right nipple. "Or Shakshouka! Something hot and rejuvenating with lots of protein."

This was getting exciting. "Yes!" I squeaked. "We can make one of those breakfast dishes that keep overnight in the refrigerator, and then you pop it into the oven in the morning. That can be the second rule; we'll make the gifts the same breakfast each time. How do we let them know they've been picked?" I paused, suddenly worried. "Suppose they turn us down? I'm not worried about fucking, I think we can figure that part out, it's the schematics of the gift acquisition that feel a little daunting."

Lucky growled into my ear, "Dykes don't turn us down, baby. Let's pick out our gift together, then we'll seduce the lucky winner."

"Dykes don't turn us down?!" I snorted. "Now you sound like an arrogant player! I don't know about you, hot stuff, but plenty of dykes have turned me down!"

Lucky laughed huskily. "Hey, this is my fantasy, and in *my* world, you and I are experts in the art of seduction. We walk into the drag king bar and elegant kings fall over themselves to buy us mocktails. We're propositioned by butches in overalls near the carrot cake platter at potlucks. Flannel-clad genderqueer activists in downtown Northampton accost us with their names and numbers rather than the latest political petition. The handsome butch plumber strips down to a tight tank top to unclog our pipes and…"

"Okay, okay, I get the picture!" I laughed, amused at Lucky's imagination. "Wait a minute. Are we being bad? Morally defunct?" I sat up straight in bed, throwing Lucky off me. Lucky bounced a little, her silver hair and breasts swaying. I was genuinely and abruptly startled at my thoughts. "Are we objectifying our friends and friends-of-friends in the worst, most misogynistic way possible?"

I shuddered as I remembered that time in the late 1970s when the wimmin's cooperative bookstore, Fan the Flames in Columbus, Ohio, had rejected my hand-printed greeting cards because I'd sexualized and objectified women in my artwork. Yes, I drew hot naked women, but I couldn't understand the 1970s lesbian feminists' issues with women's sexiness and sexuality. I'd been equally mortified and horrified; mortified because they didn't like me and horrified because I didn't like them. A little later, I'd had a long-term lover that bristled loudly whenever I admired her rounded, tempting ass. Those experiences had left me leery of offending women with my enthusiastic lechery, however that changed when I met Lucky. Lucky heartily enjoyed objectification, and my baggage surrounding sexual objectification dissipated—that is, until that very moment when The Voice of Doom was activated and started its shrill progression in my head.

Fortunately, Lucky brought me back down to earth.

"Baby, I love it when you objectify me. Listen, we're just playing and having fun." Lucky ground her cunt into my ass to emphasize her appreciation. "I think we should hand out a keepsake, a bit like winning an Olympic gold medal or an Emmy."

I mulled it over. "Or maybe more like a secret society amulet. 'I hereby ordain you into the Order of the Solstice of Pleasure with this pendant.' and we could slip it over their neck the next morning with a flourish!"

Lucky added excitedly, "The keepsake can be a key fob! We can find a jeweler on Etsy to make them up, maybe with an engraved naked lady and some fir branches!"

I giggled, "So, our Solstice Gift rules are that we have the threesome on winter solstice, the gift is only chosen once, they stay the night, we have a traditional breakfast, we give each winner a memento....are there any more rules? Do we have rules about how we fuck? How about rules on who we pick? Do you choose on odd numbered years and I choose on even numbered years, or must we have a consensus? Can one of us veto the other's choice? Are there age limits like no one younger than, say, 40?"

"These are all serious considerations. I think that we must agree wholeheartedly on our gift. No reservations. We can collect names throughout the year, add them to a Solstice Gift sheet, like a dyke version of 1950s tattoo artist Samuel Steward with his index cards of tricks, except that we're writing down names in advance rather than after it's all over. This really is the Pulitzer Prize of Dyke Threesomes," Lucky added.

"Wait, that's it!" I gave a little leap in bed, causing the sweat between my ass and Lucky's groin to slide and squeak. "We can also keep note cards for each year and maybe even a leather-bound photo album with a few pages documenting each Solstice Gift night. It would be so adorable. I'm thinking a purple padded album with our gilded monograms on the cover. I'm not sure what we'd write though. Their names and where we met them, I suppose..."

"That's all very charming and I don't mean to be crude, but don't you think we should record details of our fuck?" Lucky dryly asked. "I mean, isn't pleasure the whole point of this evil little plan, sweet cakes?"

"I suppose so...." I trailed off as I started to fall asleep. Lucky held me close, her big spoon to my little spoon.

CHAPTER THREE
Dant y Llew Helps Out

And thus it came to pass that the years and the Solstice Gifts accumulated. Each winter solstice had a unique, delicious flavor, like heirloom apples ripening on trees in autumn orchards.

We always announced the list of Solstice Gift contenders toward the end of September on the autumn equinox. When we first started the tradition, I joked that we should just nail a list of names onto a secluded tree somewhere and let the Solstice Gift contenders compete for our attention. Once that idea ignited, it grew. The first year, we commissioned a local Radical Faerie papermaker to hand craft a half ream of sheets for the announcements and associated paper accoutrements. Dant y Llew Ffyrnig (Dandelion the Fierce) was a craftsman with Welsh aspirations, a bristling blond mohawk, skintight hot pink leather pants, and a lush sing-song accent.
We nervously explained the Solstice Gift concept to him at his workshop, dancing around our mission while leaning over a display case of business card, wedding invitation, and graduation announcement samples. Dant y Llew screwed his face up in bafflement as we stammered our way through the Solstice Gift idea. Finally, Lucky gave up, leaned over the counter, and announced, *sotto voce*, "We're hosting a threesome every December and need to make invitations. Can you help us?"

Dant y Llew lit up excitedly, "Oh, wow! Now I understand! You're *Dynion Mwyn*," he proclaimed. "You'll need the paper for proclaiming the participants during the *Gwyl Canol Hydref* and the winner during the *Gwyl Canol Gaeaf*. Got it!"

I looked at Lucky discreetly and raised my eyebrow questioningly, not knowing what the hell Dant y Llew was talking about. Lucky leaned over to whisper in my ear, "I think he thinks we're pagans or witches or something."

I gathered myself together and attempted to look wise and witchy but am sure that I looked merely constipated. Looking wise was never my strong suit.

Dant y Llew hauled out a book of paper samples. "Here are the paper colors, finishes, and edges that I normally make. However, for your *Gwyl Canol Gaeaf* ritual I'd like to create something unique, something special."

After much back and forth between the three of us, we decided upon an old-fashioned lavender parchment paper with subtle gold flecks and gold deckled edges.

Each year, I laboriously wrote the contenders' names on the handmade paper. I was no calligrapher, but I was careful to make the names graceful. During the third year there was a near calamity when "Margot" was mistaken for "Margret", two highly competitive sisters, both eager to leap into our bed that December. My flowery penmanship resulted in much *mishegas* and hurt feelings. After a flurry of dramatic texts—and an afternoon at Woodstar Cafe filled with processing and teary apologies from myself to Margot and Margret—I learned my lesson; from then on out, I reined in the calligraphy flourishes and made sure that the names were completely and totally legible.

We picked a hearty oak tree on the Smith College campus near Paradise Pond and along the Mill River to hang the Solstice Gift lists. I had an overly romanticized vision of all-women's colleges. My mother had attended Mary Baldwin College in the 1950s, an all-women's college in the Blue Ridge Mountains in Staunton, Virginia. She and her classmates celebrated May 1st the traditional way, and she had the black and white photos in her yearbook to prove it. When I thought of Smith College, I had visions of women in gauzy Grecian gowns twirling around Maypoles in some kind of springtime Bacchanalian frenzy, their gowns falling onto the dew-covered grass leaving them naked, sweaty, and groping one another. A tree on Smith campus was the perfect place to post our Solstice Gift contender list.

Over the years, little offerings from each Solstice Gift contender popped up on our front porch between the autumn equinox and Pearl Harbor Day, piled up on the little red table next to our antique twig rocker. It was a sweet and unexpected addition to our annual tradition.

CHAPTER FOUR
Pooh Bear and The Longest Night, Performing the Sexual Narrative with Three Bodies

2014

2014 was the first year of the Solstice Gift tradition. Behrouz and I felt both excited and tentative. I still went through bouts of shyness and worried that the entire idea of the Solstice Gift was the grossest of juvenile objectifications, and that we'd get blow-back from our friends when they caught wind of our little idea. I supposed that we could have palmed it off as an avant-garde piece of performance art; something like "The Longest Night: Performing the Sexual Narrative With Three Bodies" or some such silliness, but I wasn't at all sure we could pull off this bit of sexual mayhem.

We spent two long midsummer weeknights during July drinking mocktails while sitting on our bentwood swing on the front porch, a smoldering mosquito coil on the side table, browsing through Etsy stores for a medallion to commemorate the Solstice Gift celebration. We finally special-ordered the *Equestris Dignitas ad Solstitium Donum* ("Order of the Solstice Gift") medallion from a women's collective in the Iowa countryside called the Rowdy Rural Renegades who were tickled pink by our newly hatched Solstice Gift tradition and promised custom work. The medallion was brass and engraved with a naked woman surrounded by three stars on one side, and the words "*Equestris Dignitas ad Solstitium Donum*" enclosed in a half wreath of pine boughs on the other side. The Renegades offered a discount for a dozen, so we ordered twelve medallions. It was hard to imagine us being pliable and energetic enough to fuck in three-ways in twelve years. In twelve years, I would be 72 and Lucky would be 62, although the older I got, the whole concept of "old" changed and moved into the future. The prospect of threesomes at age 72 was almost enough to make me start up with yoga, just to work on my already dubious agility.

We bought a plum-colored moleskin Solstice Gift notebook with metallic gold deckle-edged pages and started off with 2014 and three butches' names. It felt both monumental and a little silly to start the Solstice Gift book. In 2014, we chose between Pooh Bear, Erin Campbell, and Clarisse Savage. Pooh was a 77-year-old retired butch curator who had worked at Amherst College's Beneski Museum of Natural History. She was renowned for her taxidermy skills, along with a cool debonair panache. Erin was in her mid-40s, a therapist at the local sex therapy practice, with unruly silvery dreadlocks and a filthy sense of humor. Clarisse was a 55-year-old genderqueer UPS driver that we'd been flirting with over drag queen bingo for over a year.

Our sense of fairness nearly aborted the Solstice Gift process before it even started. We didn't want to reject Pooh, Erin, or Clarisse; they were all fine butches that we would be proud and ecstatic to have our way with. Finally, late at night, we just tossed a coin. A Susan B. Anthony dollar to be exact. It landed on heads and thus we picked the sardonic Pooh. We prepared nervously, changing the bed sheets three times before we settled on pristine white flannel. Even choosing what to make for dinner was difficult. After a week of nightly agonized menu discussions with cookbooks strewn from one end of the dining room table to the other, we finally decided upon salmon with capers, sweet potato fries, and a spinach and pear salad. Lucky remembered at the last minute that Pooh was gluten-intolerant, so we changed desert from angel food cake to lime gelato.

Pooh had style, with her shaved head and pale grey eyes. She was caramel-colored and sinewy from rock-climbing and sailing and was fond of dressing in monochrome. She showed up at our home for the Solstice celebration dressed in shades of white from head to toe; cream-colored corduroy pants, white cloth high-tops, a winter white cable-knit turtleneck wool sweater, a taupe knit cap, and a massive moonstone ring set in silver. It was snowing lightly, and white snowflakes clung to her head and shoulders as she stood in our doorway, the yellow light from inside spilling over her and the overhead porch light giving her a sparkling halo. Lucky and I were taken aback at her beauty. Pooh was a glowing apparition, radiating passion, our butch succubus for the long night. Pooh spent her retirement summers traveling the world on barges and, over a candlelit Solstice Gift supper, regaled us with spicy tales of after-hours hotel shenanigans during the infamous 1982 Barnard Conference and subsequent lesbian sex wars. After dinner, we retired to the living room where we put on some Etta James and chattered nervously, until Pooh rolled her eyes in exasperation at our nervous reticence and pounced on us.

After making out on the sofa for a few sultry songs, Pooh dragged us into our lair. Pooh ended up being surprisingly vanilla in her sexual proclivities. Her idea of a good time involved Lucky's eager tongue between Pooh's silver-haired cunt, Pooh's juices coating Lucky's cheeks until they shimmered, while I watched in gleeful voyeuristic heaven. Lucky was overjoyed to be able to indulge in her fondness for eating cunt, a proclivity that wasn't part of our coupled sexual practice. There was an element of adventure sex and of gift giving with the ritual of the Solstice Gift, a stretching beyond our usual parameters into a larger love. Later, Pooh and Lucky tag-teamed me, with me perched with Lucky's cock in my ass and Pooh's hand buried in my cunt. I adore being filled completely, and that night I came so hard that I shot come clear across the bedroom, drenching the quilt, the sheets, and Pooh's face and breasts, her nipples hard, elongated, and deep brown in the moonlight. The three of us slept intertwined and peacefully during the longest night, piled under our quilts with the snow blanketing the trees outside.

Late the next morning, Lucky and I prepared a hearty celebratory breakfast for the three of us: gluten-free cornmeal waffles with bourbon peach compote, sausage, fried green apples, and scrambled eggs, washed down with strong coffee. Pooh grinned delightedly over her waffles when we bestowed her with the brass *Equestris Dignitas ad Solstitium Donum* medallion key fob on a lavender grosgrain ribbon. We raised our coffee mugs high and toasted, "To each and every year's Solstice Gift! Long may we all reign!"

CHAPTER FIVE
Honey Campbell of Ye Olde Pull My Daisy Shoppe

2015

In 2015, we felt more adept with the Solstice gift process; at any rate we were able to make a choice without tossing a coin. We narrowed it down to a quirky genderqueer artist named Frog X who had green hair and lurid sleeve tattoos, Honey Campbell who was a red-headed florist and baker of cannabis infused goodies, and Micky Trout, a bookstore clerk and a professional clown. At one point, after a late night game of Scrabble, Lucky and I had a long tea-fueled conversation where we imagined an orgy with all five of us tangled up like a discontent skein of yarn, the kind that of yarn that changes from thick to thin every five inches and is made of a dozen kinds of fibers. It might have been interesting, but I wasn't sure if it was workable.

We fell for bribery and drugs when Honey left a wee box of pot brownies on our front porch on Halloween night, all tied up with curly black satin ribbon. Honey was a genderqueer singing florist who arranged wildflowers and succulents at Northampton's artsy florist, Ye Olde Pull My Daisy Shoppe, and who sang contralto in the local queer choral group, the Happy Valley Rainbow Singers. Honey was in their mid-30s, had silky, curly ginger hair, chubby cheeks, round hazel eyes with heavy lids, a stocky body, billowy pale thighs, and a meaty ass. Honey was passionate about horticulture and baking. They ran a cookie store on Etsy, a booming side business baking THC-infused snickerdoodle cookies that they sold under-the-table at Ye Olde Pull My Daisy, and their baked goods were a huge hit at potlucks. They were known for a generous hand with the butter and a parsimonious hand with the sugar, which made for elegantly sophisticated delicacies. Despite their baby face and innocent demeanor, Honey was a fierce top who wielded a purple leather flogger while demurely flagging red and black.

The week of solstice found us planning, plotting, and polishing. We'd spent days cooking, shining up my antique silver candelabra, and ironing and starching the table linens. We'd decided to up the game this solstice celebration by honing the celebration into the gayest holiday pagan-esque threesome ever. We'd done some sleuthing about Honey's favorite foods with their best friend, Adrian, and had cooked steak *au poivre*, creamed spinach, potato fries, and cherry clafoutis for our solstice night dinner. I was coaxing lavender candles into the silver candelabra on the dining room table as Lucky pitted cherries for the clafoutis when Francy absconded with one of the steaks, gleefully dragging it off to his dusty lair under the sideboard. Fortunately, we were both meat size queens and were able to trim one of the remaining two steaks in half.

When Honey showed up that solstice night, we were as excited and nervous as two eager bottoms-for-the-night could possibly be. Honey bounced into our home, wearing a red wool cape with a tasseled hood. They grinned with their teeth flashing white and pointed in the foyer light, looking like someone who'd escaped from the Black Forest just in time to avoid running into the wicked witch or the big bad wolf—or perhaps Honey *was* the wicked wolf! Honey's nose and cheeks were pink from the cold and they'd thoughtfully brought a napkin-lined wicker basket of small tea cakes to munch on during the night. Their purple flogger was fastened to their belt, ready for action. Lucky and I may have swooned when we opened the door. I do know that we wore vintage woolen loungewear and stood side-by-side, holding hands like two errant children waiting for a scolding. Honey wolfed down dinner cheerfully and ravenously, and even Lucky was a little intimidated by Honey's boisterous eagerness. After dinner, under Honey's sweet-natured but demanding tutelage, we retired ceremoniously to the bedroom, skipping the living room entirely.

Once in our bedroom, Honey was a jolly sadist, as quick with the giggle as they were with the flogger, and had us tied together face-to-face in no time, leaving our naked heinies exposed and Lucky's lips pressed against mine. Honey inserted a short bulbous plug into the squirming Lucky's ass then stood back to cackle and admire their work. The harder and longer Honey beat us, the more ravenous I became for Lucky. My nipples hardened against her breasts and my tongue wiggled its way into her mouth. Lucky and I were smushed together, sweaty and hot. I could feel the heat from Lucky's cunt, and tried frantically to rub my cunt against her clit. Although Lucky and I were unsuccessful with our efforts to rub our cunts together, the combination of kissing, the plug in Lucky's ass, overheated flesh, and the flogging had us both coming together quickly.

By the time Honey's lubed up hand slithered into my cunt, I was moaning, begging them to fuck me. I love getting fisted from behind; whatever spot it hits, it's one that cranks my engine, so when Honey's fist was finally buried in my cunt, I came and could not stop, my come squirting like a geyser. This set off a chain reaction of orgasms between Lucky and I, both of us yelling into the night until we were hoarse. Much later, Honey untied us and commanded Lucky to suck their clit. According to Honey, word of the dexterity of Lucky's tongue and fingers had made the rounds in the Pioneer Valley, and they wanted to find out for themself if the rumors were true. An hour and several loud orgasms later, Honey concluded that they were true. Wrung out and happy, the three of us demolished the tea cakes and then slept together in a grand puppy pile under the quilts and comforter, and the winter winds sang us to sleep.

The following morning brought a surprise. Unbeknown to us, Pooh was Honey's ex. The breakup had occurred late that autumn and the wounds were still tender. We didn't discover this *faux pas* until breakfast. I had just settled a beaming Honey into the chair of honor at the breakfast table and had served her a cup of black tea with milk. Lucky slipped the *Equestris Dignitas ad Solstitium Donum* medallion on its lavender ribbon over Honey's charmingly tussled head, tufts of red hair sticking up willy-nilly, reminders of an early morning tussle. Honey glanced down at the brass medallion nestled between their freckled breasts and burst into sobs, tears running over her plump cheeks. I felt dreadful, like we'd just harmed a rosy cherub. It took us a good half hour to coax the sordid break-up tale from Honey: passive-aggressive unreturned messages from Pooh, drunken sweaty break-up sex in the back of Pooh's pick-up truck, Honey's futile attempt at burning photos of Pooh while angrily vaping pot by the cooler at Pull My Daisy, and the finality of returned house-keys, which was the awful moment when Honey saw the *Equestris Dignitas ad Solstitium Donum* medallion on Pooh's key fob as keys were unhooked and handed over. We felt terrible for inadvertently causing any pain to Honey and learned a valuable lesson that year. We added a new rule; from then on out, we were careful to make sure there were no heartbreak or problematic exes with our new Solstice Gifts. This task was harder than it sounded; western Massachusetts was an insular community, and girlfriends traded places with one another as freely as pollen floated in the May sunshine.

CHAPTER SIX
Honey Quotes Emma Goldman at the Orphans Harvest Potluck Dinner

2016

We nearly cancelled the celebration in 2016, both of us too depressed over the year-long spate of deaths and the presidential election to even consider our solstice celebration. When Trump's infamous "pussy tape" was released in October, where he bragged "Grab them by the pussy. You can do anything," we could barely stand it. When he won the election and Leonard Cohen died in the same week, Lucky and I crashed, too stunned to think about fucking. Hell, after Trump won, the entire Pioneer Valley was in a deep, bleak state of disbelief, frantically ringing our therapists, pleading for stronger antidepressants and more appointments. By Thanksgiving, Lucky and I had given up on the Solstice Gift; it didn't seem fitting to plan something as frivolous as a holiday threesome when the country was going to hell in a handbasket. Although we decided to go ahead and host our regular annual Orphans Harvest Potluck Dinner, we were in the process of writing a tearfully apologetic letter begging off our solstice celebration to all Solstice Gift winners, and to past and present contestants. We completed the letters, stuffed them into envelopes, and mailed them off.

We had a packed house for the annual Orphans Harvest Potluck Dinner that night. Each and every past and present Solstice Gift contestant came, all of us hollow-eyed and despondent over the election. The election had divided the country; many of us had lost family members to Fox News, and holiday plans were cancelled left and right.

Over the brined turkey, cornbread stuffing, gingered cranberry sauce, mashed potatoes, pecan topped sweet potato casserole, bacony Brussels sprouts, traditional green bean casserole, three different pies, and stout gingerbread, we were firmly lectured to by the former Solstice Gift winners and contestants. They read us the riot act about tradition, family, and community. The firm talking-to culminated with Honey standing on a chair and tipsily bellowing an Emma Goldman quote over glasses of after-dinner *digestifs* and pie: "I did not believe that a Cause which stood for a beautiful ideal, for anarchism, for release and freedom from conventions and prejudice, should demand the denial of life and joy. I insisted that our Cause could not expect me to become a nun and that the movement should not be turned into a cloister. If it meant that, I did not want it. 'I want freedom, the right to self-expression, everybody's right to beautiful, radiant things.' Anarchism meant that to me, and I would live it in spite of the whole world—prisons, persecution, everything. Yes, even in spite of the condemnation of my own comrades I would live my beautiful ideal."

Honey stepped down, took a dainty swallow of her peppermint schnapps, and smiled modestly. Everyone at the potluck was stunned by Honey's impassioned speech, applauded thunderously, and decided that if Honey had taken the trouble to memorize Emma's heartfelt and revolutionary quote, then we needed to step up to the plate and fuck like our lives depended on it. We caved in.

Our intentions with the Solstice Gift had started off with little more than Lucky's and my hedonistic desires to get all of our body parts—cunts, mouths, and assholes—filled at once. Except for one three-way with a German airline stewardess that we'd met on the return trip from our honeymoon in Tehran, and Lucky's brief fling with Lola early in our relationship, we had settled into contented monogamy. We were both sexually creative and experimental, so a once a year fling sounded fun.

Although we created it to be an annual private party, after just two years it had evolved into something bigger than that. It's hard not to sound woo-woo when I try to wax on about the profound ritual that the Solstice Gift had developed into over the years. Our friends were correct, though; somehow our silliness had become a beloved community ritual, a process of expressing our sincere and dedicated lack of heteronormativity, a way of marking the seasons and, in this terrible time of Trump, even being revolutionary. The personal is political; with each annual Solstice Gift celebration, we rejoiced in the revolutionary power of sexual pleasure and rejected the patriarchy. Women in the community depended upon the Solstice Gift ritual, the sexual energy building among us until the Solstice Gift names were announced in September, then revved up from the autumn equinox until Pearl Harbor Day, and again until the longest night.

There was an element of midsummer pagan fertility rituals to the several month long Solstice Gift process, but I was also reminded of more ordinary community building that I'd participated in creating, such as a queer open mic that I started a few years before and a quarterly LGBTQ+ comics zine that Lucky founded two years earlier. Through actions, our community is strengthened, and individual creativity is fostered. Was the Solstice Gift process so different?

At some point early on, the Solstice Gift also became service from Lucky and me to the individual Solstice Gift winners. We strove to provide each beloved Solstice Gift their intimate heart's desire, snooping with their friends, meeting them for meals and conversation, exchanging paper letters, a tender courtship leading up to the winter solstice and the longest night.

CHAPTER SEVEN
Penny Posy and the Frisky Bunny Diorama

2016

We could barely concentrate on the Solstice Gifts in 2016, what with so many deaths and the ugliness of the electoral process grinding us up like hamburger meat. We lackadaisically picked three lovely butches, Penny Posy, Smokey Bayer, and Anne Watchmaker. It was difficult to get excited after Trump was elected, but whenever we became too depressed to move, we thought of Honey and Emma Goldman. Early in December in 2016, and by the overly dramatic light of nine flickering candles in our living room, we chose Penny Posy.

Penny was originally from New Jersey. She had a thick, working class, New Jersey accent and was a butch groundskeeper at one of the five colleges, with a fondness for outsider artist installations. She was Amazonian, tall and muscular, with squinty dark brown eyes and thick black hair laced with grey along the sides. Her muscular, down-covered arms were covered with blackwork tattoos, mostly old-fashioned sailor imagery: nautical stars and swallows on her forearms, anchors on her biceps, and thick knotted rope around both wrists. We liked the dissonance between Penny's rough trade exterior and her artistic inner life, and after an intense fifteen minutes of the three of us smooching in Penny's fairy-light lit backyard one muggy midsummer night, surrounded by blinking fireflies and fragrant honeysuckle, we were also smitten with Penny's agile hands and talented tongue.

Penny had followed in Honey's footsteps when she left an elaborate handmade diorama on our front porch a few days after Halloween. It depicted a bedroom for horny lesbian bunnies, complete with three tiny felted bunnies cavorting in a carved wooden four-poster bed, and miniature renditions of Georgia O'Keefe flower paintings and framed Victorian mourning jewelry braids on the walls. One felted bunny had a little pink tongue, and all three bunnies had breasts and delicate pink vulvas with mohair pubic hair. She'd even made a heart-shaped braided rug out of yarn.

After we nailed the missive to the tree on Pearl Harbor Day letting Penny know that she was that year's Solstice Gift, there was a flurry of texts and meetings over coffee. Penny shyly admitted through text—that anonymous medium of true confessions—that despite her sturdy butch demeanor, she secretly yearned to bottom and rarely got those needs met. What better night to meet unmet desires than the longest night of the year!

That solstice night with Penny was long and luscious; we started with a simple dinner of stuffed rabbit, green beans *almondine*, a salad, and crème caramel. We didn't make it into bed until 3:00 a.m.; instead, the three of us tumbled from the sofa onto the Persian carpet in front of the wood-burning stove in the living room, buttons unbuttoning, jeans unzipping, shoelaces untying, our clothing strewn from one end of the sofa to the sideboard. Lucky and I had planned to tie up Penny as tightly as that roast bunny that we'd had for dinner, but the impromptu make-out session in the living room threatened to sidetrack our nefarious plans. Domesticity is the mother of invention, so I grabbed the drapery tieback cords for makeshift bondage. Penny looked adorably fetching by candlelight, trussed up in purple silk tiebacks and spread out immobile on the rug, the golden light from the wood-burning stove flickering over the three of us as she tossed and turned in mock agony.

That night we had our way with Penny several times over, leaving her happily sobbing, bruised, and starry-eyed. Later, during postcoital snuggles, Penny confessed that the diorama's Victorian framed mourning jewelry was actually made from her braided pubic hair. Lucky and I were both impressed with Penny's dedication to art and fucking. When Penny offered to make us a miniature framed art piece with our braided pubic hair. I was intrigued and Lucky politely demurred, but we finally agreed to commission one from Penny made of our combined pubic hair to hang next to the bed, a reminder of the importance of the perseverance of pleasure over politics. The next morning, with snow falling like angel's tears in the faint morning light, I anointed Penny with the *Equestris Dignitas ad Solstitium Donum* medallion over breakfast. As tradition dictated, we raised our coffee mugs high over the groaning table of food and toasted, "To each and every year's Solstice Gift! Long may we all reign!" We were all a little teary-eyed as we remembered the longest night that exceedingly difficult year.

CHAPTER EIGHT
Leroy King and the Triple Daddies

2017

Picking the Solstice Gift for 2017 turned out to be easy-peasy. That was the year that our ancient Subaru Forester, Ruby Tuesday, finally shuddered to a halt and nearly went into the Subaru graveyard in the sky, but we decided to put in a last-ditch effort to get it repaired. The owners of the shop we'd been going to, Gay's Gearhead NoHo Car Repair, had retired, so we asked around for a new mechanic. The consensus was that King's Automobile Services was the cat's meow. King's Automobile Services' slogan was "King's: Where queens are kings, kings are queens, and service reigns!", and they were known for a series of peppy commercials that featured the owner, a dapper stud named Leroy King. Leroy looked to be in her mid-50s, had greying dreadlocks, a fondness for wearing a forest green bandana as a neckerchief, ironed grey mechanic's overalls with "King's" embroidered in curly red script across her chest, deep-set dark eyes behind retro black eyeglasses, and a sparkling gold labrys inlaid in one of her front teeth.

Of course, we had other contenders, but Lucky and I were totally crushed out on Leroy and the others faded into the background like distant stars to Leroy, a luminous full moon. Yeah, we had it bad and this is how it went down.

When Lucky and I saw Leroy's commercials and her series of do-it-yourself videos for the community, instructing folks how to do simple maintenance like change their car's oil, replace a gasket, winterize their car, and change a tire, all narrated by the effervescent Leroy, we swooned. Hell, half the dykes in the Valley were nefariously plotting on how to get into Leroy's spotless mechanic's overalls. We'd seen Leroy looking confidently dapper at local parties and events but hadn't had the chance to introduce ourselves to her, just admired her from across various rooms. She excluded a calm, Daddy energy and was kind and handsome, always ready with a grin, a friendly shoulder, and a hug. Leroy swaggered into Hors D'oeuvres' Drag Brunch, So's Yer Grandma polka concerts, and library fundraiser book sales with equal finesse and confidence, with her jaunty bow tie and gold labrys flashing as she laughed.

In July, we had Ruby Tuesday towed into King's Automobile Services and worriedly turned over the dear old Forester. Leroy was gentle as she let us down, explaining that it might be time to let go and get a new car. She pointed out that Ruby had over 310,000 miles on her and extensive salt corrosion in her undercarriage, then went over the repairs that would be needed to bring poor Ruby up to snuff. The three of us had a moment of silence at Ruby Tuesday's front grill, eyes downcast over the ancient metal car. We threw caution to the wind and asked Leroy out for coffee, then, when that went well, for dinner.

The months flew by; on the autumn equinox, we nailed the list of Solstice Gift finalists to the oak tree near Paradise Pond, and that year we invited Leroy to our annual Orphans Harvest Potluck Dinner for the first time. Leroy arrived with an abundance of sweet potato dishes: a scrumptious

Pyrex casserole dish of orange halves that had been stuffed with mashed sweet potatoes and topped with the obligatory miniature marshmallows, along with southern sweet potato pies. When Leroy toasted the marshmallows of the orange and sweet potato dish with a blowtorch at the dinner table, with the sleeves of her pink dress shirt rolled up, our hearts melted as surely as the marshmallows. Leroy's front porch gift to us was a whimsical wooden carved and painted replica of the dearly departed Ruby Tuesday, along with a quart of premium motor oil. Sentimentality combined with practicality; Leroy was one fine Daddy.

Leroy was a Daddy and a mechanic. She liked to fix things, tinker until everything worked just so and purred along happily, whether it was a car or a girl. Like all accomplished Daddies, Leroy had a sure touch and an intuitive nature. There was a bit of the paternal or maternal to Leroy, a soothing selflessness. I once knew a ferocious butch top who admitted dejectedly that she had a secret craving to be nurtured by someone who would take care of her instead of her doing all of the planning and the care-giving. She said that being a Daddy was exhausting, and at the same time admitted that topping was so habitual that she wasn't even sure she'd be able to accept it if someone offered to nurture her instead. Lucky and I thought of that top when we considered our plans for Leroy. What was Leroy's deepest unmet need? How could a bone-tired Daddy be nourished on the longest night? Having Leroy daddy us for the night was too obvious and would leave the three of us sated and content, but we wanted something special. In a flash of hot cider and pumpkin donut fueled inspiration, Lucky and I decided to throw a solstice slumber party for Leroy, the most Daddy Solstice Gift ever.

When Leroy knocked on our door on Thursday, December 21st, we were gleeful in anticipation. Leroy stood gallantly on the front porch in her leather jacket, black turtleneck, and button-fly jeans. The snow swirled around her, a bouquet of crimson and lavender roses in hand. We drew Leroy inside to the warmth of the living room, removed her jacket for her, and settled her into the low velvet armchair next to the glass-fronted wood-burning stove. Lucky arranged the roses in a vase, while I poured the three of us pre-dinner ginger mocktails.

We'd set the table with a red tablecloth that was printed with white snowflakes and bordered with snowmen, peppermint striped napkins, a runner edged in gold ric-rac adorned with Santa Claus in his sleigh and all the reindeer flying through the night air, and a collection of vintage Santa Claus ceramic candle holders, each holding a red lit candle. Lucky had strung paper chains from the center overhead light fixture to the corners of the dining room in an "X".

We'd done some sleuthing with a couple of Leroy's exes and had cooked her favorite childhood comfort meal of fried chicken, baked macaroni and cheese, collard greens with flavored with ham, and peach pie topped with ice cream. Leroy was astonished as Lucky brought out dinner and set it on the table, rubbing her hands together in glee and laughing. Waiting on Leroy's empty dinner plate was a tiny parchment scroll tied with gold ribbon. Lucky and I leaned forward as she unwrapped it, holding our breaths.

Golden glitter spilled out of the scroll onto her lap as Leroy unwound the invite and read the message out loud: "Dearest Leroy—You are cordially invited to the Holly Jolly Solstice Gift Longest Night Slumber Party. Please say yes!! Love, your very best Daddies, Daddy Behrouz and Daddy Lucky. P.S. We were told that Dasher, Dancer, Prancer, Vixen, Comet, Cupid, Donner, Blitzen, and Rudolph will be flying by!" Leroy looked up, pumped her fist into the air, and shouted an enthusiastic, "Yes! How did you know that I love Christmas? This is perfect!" Her eyes were gleaming with excitement, and dinner commenced.

It was a festive night. After dinner, we all changed into pajamas. Lucky and I had bought matching fuzzy onesie footie pajamas for each of us, in Scandinavian prints of red and white with reindeer and snowflakes. We lit the woodstove in the living room and put Burl Ives' *Have a Holly Jolly Christmas* on the hi-fi. We strung cranberries and popcorn by the soft glow of the fire, then pulled on snow boots and ran outside under the pale light of the waxing crescent moon and festooned the pine tree with the garlands so that the birds would have a treat. We romped in our pajamas in the snow and threw snowballs until we were too chilly. Once inside again, we played a few boisterous rounds of Chutes and Ladders and Candyland, and then finally snuggled up together on the sofa with a giant wooden bowl of buttered popcorn and steaming mugs of hot cocoa to watch *The Princess Bride* and the 1951 version of *A Christmas Carol*.

At one point, I gave Leroy a manicure, dipped her hands in a paraffin bath, softened her calluses, trimmed her cuticles, and finally painted each fingernail bright blue. As the Spirit of Christmas Present showed Scrooge how "men of goodwill" celebrate Christmas, Lucky gave Leroy a scalp massage, rubbing her scalp with lavender scented coconut oil as she groaned with pleasure and release. As the Spirit of Christmas Yet to Come visited Scrooge, we gave Leroy a green tea facial, steamed her skin with hot towels, applied a creamy green tea mask, let it do its magic, and then tenderly washed it off. 3:00 a.m. found the three of us droopy-eyed, stuffed with popcorn and ice cream, and smelling of lavender and essential oils. The cats snoozed at our feet. We toddled off to bed, climbed between the forest green flannel sheets, each of us with a stuffed velour reindeer tucked under one arm, snuggled up together in a happy puppy pile, and were snoring within seconds.

The next morning was magical. We could see the birds clustered around the pine tree with the popcorn and cranberry garlands, chirping excitedly to one another as they devoured their holiday breakfast. Lucky insisted upon serving breakfast while wearing antlers, and when she caught Leroy looking at them longingly, found another pair and crowned Leroy too. As a result, the *Equestris Dignitas ad Solstitium Donum* medallion on its lavender ribbon was bestowed upon a giggling, dread-locked reindeer in a flannel onesie that year. It seemed impossible that we could eat another meal after last night's feast, but we managed. Over breakfast, we raised our red coffee mugs high and toasted, "To each and every year's Solstice Gift! Long may we all reign!"

CHAPTER NINE
Marilyn Shoemaker and the Five Colleges

2018

In 2018, by the time the dust had settled, we chose Marilyn Shoemaker even although the whole process ended up being quite the conundrum that year. Somehow, we managed to pick one woman from each of the five colleges, Smith, Hampshire, Mount Holyoke, Amherst, and UMass Amherst. Five was way more than we normally chose. In the previous years, we'd narrowed it down to three or so, but we overextended ourselves, bit off more than we could chew, all those sad tired sayings about perfectionists and overachievers. Maybe it was because the time period leading up to the actual 2018 winter solstice felt so disassociated and eerie due to the shit show of a political and cultural situation in the States that we went hog wild and chose so many possible Solstice Gifts. We narrowed it down to Marilyn who taught gender and film studies at Smith, Ida who taught literature at Hampshire, Thom who taught art history at Mount Holyoke, Mina who taught philosophy at Amherst, and Jeanne who taught anthropology at UMass Amherst—all brilliant and handsome butches. We didn't realize that they were all professors, one from each of the five colleges until we wrote out the proclamation in September. It was a Sunday night, we were nearly done with our chores and winding down the weekend.

Lucky starched and ironed her dress shirts for the work week, and I was at the dining room table with a dessert plate of sweet potato pie, the Solstice Gift journal, a couple of pieces of our special handmade paper, and a fountain pen filled with green ink, prepared to write out everyone's names.

I blinked in dismay. "Oh fuck! Do you realize that we've chosen one from each college? Do you think this will be an issue?"

Lucky put down the iron and wandered over to the table. She took a forkful of my sweet potato pie and read the list of names over my shoulder, "Oh, honey. I don't know about this." Lucky shook her head in dismay. "It could become…"

"…competitive!" we whispered in unison.

"Green fucking monkey dicks," I muttered. "Fucking lesbians. You just know that if one dyke makes a loaf carrot cake, the next dyke will make a two-layer carrot cake with cream cheese frosting, the third one will make a three-layer carrot cake with cream cheese frosting and those cute orange carrot decorations, and the fourth will make a four-layer carrot cake with bourbon-spiked cream cheese frosting, fancy-ass piping, and edible gold leaf. It never stops."

"You are such a cranky-pants," Lucky chided me. "It is kind of funny that we have one from each college, though. Maybe we could start a Solstice Gift alumni association. Yearbooks and trophies!" Lucky kissed me. "Baby cakes, I think we're overreacting. It'll be fine. Marilyn, Thom, Mina, Jeanne, and Ida are all grown-up women. They can handle it."

We were oh, so wrong. We posted the list of Solstice Gift names on the traditional oak tree near Paradise Pond late at night on Thursday September 21st. We tip-toed and giggled through the woods hand-in-hand wearing our plaid wool jackets and toting a flask of hot cider.

By the following Sunday, our front porch was deluged with handmade chapbooks from each contestant, presenting herself as the most worthy of consideration for the Solstice Gift celebration.

Marilyn's chapbook was a thoughtful essay that argued for the presence of conceptual earth-based rebirth and trigender sexual identity within the context of ritual sex magic.

Ida's chapbook looked back at historic literary lesbian threesomes in the 1920s and 30s in Paris.

Thom left an erotic flip-book of delightfully filthy comic drawings of our imagined threesome.

Mina's chapbook was written in white ink on black paper and invoked Foucault, English boarding schools, canes, and obscure quotes in French; I made out *"L'important, c'est que le sexe n'ait pas été seulement affaire de sensation et de plaisir, de loi ou d'interdiction, mais aussi de vrai et de faux,"* in Mina's cramped cursive, but was bewildered as to its application to a threesome.

Jeanne's chapbook argued that in the current postmodern intellectual climate, and with the Solstice Gift process and ceremony, the concept of "family" had been deconstructed, the patriarchal nuclear family destroyed, a redistribution of the perimeters of the echo-familial system ignited, and reborn into a matrilineal community family grouping with Lucky and I as conjugal matriarchs, and queer sexuality as the infinite locus.

We spread the chapbooks out on our dining room table that Sunday night, read through them one-by-one, and discussed them over a pot of steaming ginger tea and a plate of salted walnut shortbread cookies. In the end, the beautiful little art books made no difference as to whom we picked, but it did allow us a horrifying glimpse at the competitive nature of academics when confronted with fucking and publication. It certainly made me look at that saying for scholars "Publish or perish" in a whole new light.

After all the *mishegas* with the chapbooks, we decided upon Marilyn. We'd happily bottomed to the adorably bouncy Honey in 2016, wanted to flip the cards, and Marilyn's cards were the ones we wanted to flip. Her intellectual smarty-pants severity was just the ticket for the longest night. Marilyn was smart, severe, sarcastic, and sexy...all the fun s's.

In addition to her career as a gender and film studies professor at Smith, the local hoity-toity women's college, Marilyn was known for her unforgiving grading, her immaculate expectations, and her obsession with the film director, David Lynch. She was the leader of a motley group of academics that were enamored with Lynch's cult movie, *Blue Velvet*. They called themselves The Lumberton Velvets, and were known for their annual sing-along screening of *Blue Velvet* at the VFW in Florence, complete with goodie bags. Even among The Lumberton Velvets, Marilyn stood out in her frank dedication to *Blue Velvet* and had memorized great chunks of the film. I was also a huge *Blue Velvet* fan, so Marilyn's love of the movie was a bonus. There was something about her stern demeanor that turned us both into big bad top Daddies, made us want to gang up on her, and demolish her until she was a puddle of come and pleasure. Marilyn, for her part, was eager and game.

Marilyn had once proclaimed haughtily, while a group of us were having a late afternoon Her Majesty's Coronation Special High Tea at The Copper Kettle Tea Room and demolishing a tiered china server of a gluttonous number of delicacies, including cucumber sandwiches, egg mayonnaise with cress sandwiches, pink smoked salmon with cream cheese sandwiches, ladylike chicken salad sandwiches, sultana-studded scones with rhubarb jam and local clotted cream, hazelnut mousse, apple-pear tatin, and ginger sponge cake, that she played within the guidelines of "risk-aware consensual kink". We were talking about old guard leather traditions, a new BDSM women's and trans play party that had just started up in Boston, Marilyn had just eaten one of the mousses and was delicately washing it down with a generous glass of rosé Champagne when she said, "I've been an exemplary masochist for over three decades and would be insulted if a top asked me for a safe word, and those fucking BDSM checklists! Don't even get me started!" I nudged Lucky under the linen-covered table and covered my smile with a napkin. Lucky and I knew that we were going to pick Marilyn for the Solstice Gift, so the fact that Marilyn disliked safe words was immensely valuable information.

On the night of the solstice, Thursday, December 21st, we picked up Marilyn at her loft in the Easthampton brick mill building in a loaned out black 1968 Dodge Charger. We'd borrowed the Charger from one of the The Lumberton Velvets, and it was a lovingly restored duplicate of the one used in *Blue Velvet*. The three of us had planned the abduction and the general tone of the night in advance, although Marilyn didn't know what nefarious *Blue Velvet*-tinged escapades we had up our well-tailored sleeves. Lucky and I wore severe vintage dark suits, white shirts, fedoras, woolen overcoats, brogues, and neckties. In a letter, we'd instructed Marilyn to wear grey flannel trousers, a black turtleneck, low boots, and no underwear. We arrived fifteen minutes late in order to allow the punctual and driven professor to stew, driving up cooly and slowly in the dark winter night. Marilyn was waiting for us outside, tapping her booted toe impatiently. I was driving, so I let the engine idle as I waited in the car.

Marilyn greeted Lucky, then glanced at her watch, "Hi there. Nice wheels. Was there a problem getting over here?"

Lucky bounded out and grabbed Marilyn, twisted her arm behind her back, and hissed menacingly, "Don't you fucking look at me!" Marilyn jumped, startled. "Your safe word is 'I finger banged Andrea Dworkin!' Say it!" Lucky growled.

Marilyn flushed angrily, clearly trying to decide if she could cave in, follow our directions, and say the dreaded sentence. A couple of moments passed, but finally Marilyn closed her eyes in resignation, gave a deep sigh and whispered, "I finger banged Andrea Dworkin."

"Louder!" I yelled out the window from the driver's seat. "I can't hear you!"

Marilyn gritted her teeth. "I finger banged Andrea Dworkin," she said in a normal voice.

"Still can't hear you. Speak up!" I yelled again.

"I finger banged Andrea Dworkin?" Marilyn pleaded with Lucky.

Lucky grabbed Marilyn by her sweater and hissed menacingly, "My wife wants to hear you say, 'I finger banged Andrea Dworkin.' You can talk, right? Now say it so Behrouz can hear it!" she commanded.

"I finger banged Andrea Dworkin!" Marilyn yelled, her words echoing around the snow-covered parking lot and brick buildings. She winced as she heard the despised sentence in the still winter night.

"That's better." Lucky sniffed the cold night air. "Do I smell cigar smoke?" she demanded as she spied a still smoldering cigar butt in the snow.

Marilyn's eyes grew big and dark, and she stammered, "But you were late, and I was waiting…"

"We. Are. Never. Late," Lucky growled into Marilyn's ear, then slapped her cheek, spun her around, snapped faux fur-lined leather cuffs on her, tied a blindfold around her head, opened the back door, and tossed the professor in like a bag of unruly potatoes.

Lucky slammed the door extra hard, winked at me, climbed into the front passenger seat, and we prepared to drive around town for a little over an hour. Marilyn needed to stew, the car needed washing, we needed another bottle of lube from Oh My Sensuality Shop, Francy and Bear were out of cat food, and I had ordered a book from Broadside Bookshop that was ready to be picked up. We went to Oh My first and bought a sparkly, festive gold silicone butt plug on a whim.

Once back in the Charger, but while we were still in the parking garage and with last minute Christmas shoppers streaming by our darkened car and "Here Comes Santa Claus" piped in on the overhead speakers, Lucky unzipped Marilyn's flannel pants, pulled them partially down, inserted the golden plug into Marilyn's twitching asshole, then pulled her pants back up and slapped her ass, forcing the plug in deeper. Lucky leaned over Marilyn's prone, trussed up body, pulled her turtleneck away from her neck and bit that throbbing expanse of delicate flesh. "Let's hit the fuckin' road, we're givin' our neighbor a joy ride," Lucky snarled maniacally. Marilyn moaned through her gag.

"Now that our little friend has a golden plug up her greedy ass, let's take this pussy wagon to the streets and find a matching golden nozzle!" Lucky gloated.

"Baby, we're going to fill you with cock and come until you can't stand up anymore!" I chortled, feeling like a character in *Blue Velvet* as I squealed the tires rounding a corner as sharply as I could. I heard a happy whimper from the back seat.

We drove to the Golden Nozzle Car Wash, all the while making crass juvenile jokes about nozzles and golden showers. We enjoyed every moment of Marilyn's obvious discomfort, then pulled into the brick building with a sharp right turn which tossed Marilyn about in the back seat. Lucky rummaged in the bowling bag at her feet for a minute until she found the next implements in our wicked plan. She held up a pair of tit clamps in one hand and a large remote-controlled bullet vibrator in the other.

Lucky opened the back door again, and yanked up Marilyn's turtleneck, tweaking her already hard nipples. And she moaned, her hips arching upward with need. We could hear traffic drive by; after all, it was a just a few days before Christmas and people were out shopping and admiring the lights. "Hey neighbor, are you ready to have some fun?" Lucky fastened a clamp to Marilyn's left breast, pulled on it, fastened the right one, and then gently pulled her top down, unzipped her slacks, and reached down to finger Marilyn's cunt. "What have we here? No panties, and you've left a big wet come stain on the crotch of your flannels already. You're very messy for being such a brainiac." Lucky started jerking Marilyn off rubbing on either side of her swollen clit, but stopped just as she was about to come, then slid the bullet into Marilyn's soaked cunt and pulled her slacks back up. "Now, we're going to clean up this pussy wagon!"

We took our time in the Golden Nozzle. We'd splurged on an Unlimited Wash Plan 4 Interior and Exterior earlier that year, so we wanted to take full advantage of the membership. Midway through the wash, Lucky started playing with the remote control on the vibrator. I'd never had much luck with little bullet vibrators, preferring the supersonic blast of the magic wand, but judging from the gasps and moans coming from the back seat, Marilyn seemed to be enjoying it.

I cranked up The Runaways on the CD player, and we drove through the wash bay, leisurely treating the borrowed Charger to suds and a wax. By the time we came out the other side, Lucky and I were singing along to "Cherry Bomb" and the car looked better than it'd looked since Jimmy's 529 Club Cruise last September. We both got out so that we could detail the tires and peeked in on Marilyn.

"How are you doing back there?" I asked.

Marilyn whined, "I can't come! I'm not used to little vibrators like this one. I need a wand to come!"

"Look, neighbor," Lucky yanked Marilyn out of the car. "Who the fuck said you were allowed to come?" Marilyn started to protest.

"It's cold out here. When are we going to your place?" she whined impatiently.

"Aw, you're being too hard on the professor." I put my arm around Marilyn and pulled her blindfold up so that she could see where we were.

Marilyn looked from Lucky to me, then to the nearby road where last-minute shoppers rushed by. "People might see us!" she wailed.

"Don't you fucking talk to me. We're your neighbors!" Lucky slapped Marilyn across her face, hard. "Do you need your safe word now? Want us to stop?"

"No!" A panicked Marilyn sputtered.

I twisted the tit clamps through Marilyn's sweater, "'No' what? 'No', stop it? Okay, we'll stop." I let go and stepped back a foot.

"I mean, no don't stop! I'm sorry," Marilyn pleaded.

Lucky grabbed Marilyn's cunt through her trousers. "I think you really do need your safe word. Let's practice now. Say it."

"I finger banged Andrea Dworkin," Marilyn said. "Please…"

"Baby, it's late. We need to go home now." I threw Marilyn into the back seat again, got into the Charger, and looked back at her. "Marilyn, you are not being compliant. I think you need to practice your safe word. It's a fifteen-minute drive to our home. I want to hear you say, 'I finger banged Andrea Dworkin' the entire way home."

Lucky laughed, "Marilyn, you know how some teachers make their students write 'I will not misbehave in class' 500 times on the blackboard? I've heard all about what a hardass you are. Think of this as much justified comeuppance. Now, start talking."

Lucky and I drove home to a chorus of "I finger banged Andrea Dworkin," on endless repeat. Marilyn started off resigned, then barreled through contrite and angry. We took the long way home, slowing down to admire gloriously gaudy Christmas light arrangements and, by the time we got home, she sounded desperate. We pulled up into our driveway and fetched Marilyn from the back seat.

"How many times did you say it?" I asked her.

Marilyn's eyes filled with tears. "I don't know," she stammered.

"Aw baby. What do you mean you don't know?"

"I'm sorry, but I didn't know you wanted me to keep count," she looked at both of us pleadingly.

Lucky shook her head sadly, reached into her bowling bag that was on the passenger seat floor, brought out a wooden sorority paddle, then slapped her hand with it lightly. She said, slowly, "I'm extremely disappointed in you, Marilyn." I opened the front door to our house, then Lucky pushed Marilyn into the warmth of our home, through the foyer, and into the living room. We yanked Marilyn's slacks down, bent her over the sofa, and admired Marilyn's unmarked ass. I winked at Lucky.

"Now, let's see how many times you can say 'I finger banged Andrea Dworkin' in the next sixteen minutes. You'd better keep count this time!" I warned the squirming professor. I set my phone's timer for eight minutes, and Lucky took the first hit on Marilyn's tush. Lucky beat her for the first eight minutes, we reset the timer, and I paddled her for the second eight minutes.

By the time the sixteen- minute beating was over with, Marilyn's ass was bright red and she was crying and pleading with us, tears and snot running down her cheeks. "I finger banged Andrea Dworkin three hundred and eighty-five," she blubbered. "I'm sorry. I'm so, so sorry. I'll behave from now on. I promise."

Lucky reached down, parted Marilyn's cunt lips, and slid her hand into the professor's soaking wet cunt where it fit like an elderly lady's thin, fine leather glove—snug and well loved, like they were made for each other, molded into one another's shape. Come was already dripping down Marilyn's leg as she arched her hips upwards to urge Lucky's hand in deeper inside her cunt.

Watching Lucky fist our helpless friend was hot as fuck, so I unzipped my jeans, pulled them partway down, laid an antimacassar over the seat of the green velvet armchair, and settled down to jerk off. My clit was red and engorged, protruding between my cunt lips, and I was soaking wet. I tugged on my aching flesh, imagining Lucky's hand inside of me. I loved being filled by Lucky, and I loved watching her fill another person. By the time I came, the professor was yelling, Lucky was growling, and the cats were hiding.

I'd sunk deep into the armchair's overstuffed cushions, so I hauled myself up with some difficulty, pulled up my pants, and went over to help Marilyn. I unfastened the cuffs from her wrists and wrapped her up with a wool lap quilt. Lucky and I hugged for her a few minutes, then I broke free to go into the kitchen and start dinner.

Lucky and I had made *Ghormeh sabzi* (Persian herb stew) in the slow cooker earlier in the day and it was still there, staying warm, so now all I needed to do was to steam some basmati rice. I was measuring out the rice into the electric rice cooker, when Lucky and Marilyn wandered into the kitchen. Lucky sat Marilyn down at the kitchen table and came over to pour us all tumblers of sparkling water. Dinner was lovely; we'd made *Ghormeh sabzi* for a dinner party last spring and Marilyn had been enamored of its unique blend of sweet and sour. After dinner, we took bowls of split brownies topped with cardamom vanilla ice cream into the living room and stayed up watching the lesbian classic *Mädchen in Uniform*. Francy and Bear lounged contentedly over us, purring madly, happy that we had finally stopped bellowing and were doing our job which was to feed them and pet their furry bellies. Marilyn admitted to being impressed with all the *Blue Velvet* references throughout the night and was mulling over writing a publication incorporating *Blue Velvet*, a history of Victorian and 20th century lesbian BDSM sexual practices, Dorothy Valance's feminist evolution, and Lincoln's assassination. By the time the three of us got to sleep curled up together under the down comforter, it was snowing hard again, and the outdoor temperature had fallen into the teens for the longest night.

When we bestowed the order of the *Equestris Dignitas ad Solstitium Donum* on its lavender ribbon to Marilyn at the breakfast table the following morning, she blushed prettily then dug into the cornmeal waffles with an appetite honed by the Golden Nozzle, Andrea Dworkin, and some unfortunate sorority girl's wooden paddle. With Roy Orbison crooning "In Dreams" from the hi-fi, we raised our coffee mugs high over the linen tablecloth and toasted, "To each and every year's Solstice Gift! Long may we all reign!"

PART TWO: THE PRESENT

CHAPTER TEN
The Solstice Gift Choices

Summer, 2019

Each summer, Lucky begins the solstice discussion and I follow. We've been doing it for five years now, so we have the routine down pat. This year it started like this: Lucky opened the Sunday morning newspaper, the smoky scent of ink rising into the air, and sniffed, "Look, the new librarian is in the newspaper! Her name is Flynn." She showed me a picture of a smiling librarian standing next to a Pride book display. There was a rainbow made of cut-up felt on the bulletin board behind the books, and the librarian looked familiar. I thought I'd seen her at the food co-op, filling a green glass jar with extra virgin olive oil. She was handsome, with her short chestnut curly hair, round glasses, tight jeans, plaid shirt, and chukka boots. Lucky said, "Let's add her to the Solstice Gift list. I think that she has a certain studious *je ne sais quoi* quality about her, plus a delightful ass."

I wiped a smear of butter from my fingers to the napkin, then reached across the table to pour Lucky a little more hot tea. "She's cute and all, but what about the shy silver fox that we saw at Marilyn's potluck last Saturday? The boyish one who brought the strawberry-rhubarb pie and works at Broadside Bookshop. I liked her. Is she in the Solstice Gift book yet?"

I blushed, remembering how I'd flirted with her as we dipped our pita triangles into the obligatory garlicky hummus.

"Yes, her name is Trixie and I added her. Darling, I do believe you have a thing for silver-haired butches," Lucky smirked as she winked at me over the fat-bellied teapot and freshened her tea.

In July, we added Ebony's second cousin, Raven, to the Solstice Gift list. Raven was in her early 60s, shaved her head, and was fond of dressing like the construction worker from the 1970s disco group The Village People. Lucky and I argued about whether this was dipping into the honeypot too close to home, so to speak, but Ebony was still living in the Bay Area, so we figured we ran a very small chance of any weirdness.

In early August, I talked Lucky into adding an older long-haired butch named Sheila that I knew from the Pie Bar in Florence. Sheila was a pastry chef at the Pie Bar with a sly, knowing squint, a rangy build, and long greying braids. Lucky didn't know Sheila but became convinced of her suitability after I invited Sheila to one of our potlucks, where she wowed us with lemon pie and a fine recitation of the Victorian satirical poem and cautionary tale by Hilaire Belloc, "Matilda Who told Lies, and was Burned to Death."

Later in August, we added a bouncy, sturdy, pocket butch named Scout to the Solstice Gift list. Scout was in her late 50s, with round cobalt blue spectacles and thick, short greying hair. She was a part-time custom picture framer at Frame-Up or Else, but her true love was sweets. Scout was a chocolatier, selling her dainties to co-ops, confectioneries, and small-batch artisan food shops throughout New England. Scout played accordion with a band called So's Yer Grandma, which consisted of a group of seven queer, rambunctious, malcontent punks. They were often found squeezing the box at the local queer polka dances. In May at the Northampton Pride Parade,

So's Yer Grandma had caused a minor furor by dressing up in matching rainbow kilts and marching in the parade topless, while playing a rowdy rendition of "I Will Survive." They announced that they were there to fight fascism, damn it!

And so it went, adding up possible gifts until we had a stack entered into the plum-colored moleskin Solstice Gift notebook. We stuck a little photo, held in place with little triangular black paper photo corners, next to each woman's entry along with notes about their hobbies, where we knew them from, any known sexual proclivities, whether we'd fucked any of their exes, and who was exes with whom. These were important details, particularly the last one, as we had discovered rather dramatically with Honey on the morning of December 22nd, 2015.

CHAPTER ELEVEN
An Unseasonably Warm Night

September 22nd and 23rd, 2019

By September of 2019, we'd collected a list of five Solstice Gifts. There was Flynn Baldwin, the cataloging librarian with a fine ass; Ebony's second cousin, Raven Woods, who was a stand-up comic during Queer Bang-Up Open Mic at The Deuce and was fond of dressing like the construction worker from the old disco group The Village People; an older long-haired butch named Sheila Willis with braids and a sly, knowing squint who baked pies over at the Pie Bar in Florence; an energetic and bouncy pocket butch named Scout Müller with round cobalt blue spectacles who played accordion at the local queer polka dances; and Trixie Trout, the flirtatious silver fox and bookseller from Marilyn's summer holiday potluck.

On Sunday night, September 22nd, I found myself laboriously writing the names of the Solstice Gift contenders onto lavender parchment while Lucky polished her boots. It was unseasonably warm that night and we were both grumbling about the heat wave. We were in the kitchen with the windows open, hoping that the faint night breeze would help. Francy and Bear were stretched out on the cool tiled floor, sleeping and with their furry bellies exposed. I took another swig of iced blackberry tea. "Fuck climate change. It feels strange to be writing out the Solstice Gift names in this heat."

Lucky got out her phone to look up monthly weather patterns for Northampton. "Today's high was 15 degrees warmer than average. And it doesn't look like it's going to cool down until October, so tomorrow night will be warm again."

"Piss," I grumbled, as I distractedly smeared the ink on "Flynn," crumpled up the paper, and started fresh.

That night we slept under just a thin cotton sheet and woke up to iced coffee instead of hot coffee, as we had been doing all month.

On Monday, September 23rd we gathered our supplies. After so many years of doing this, we had a ritual. Lucky wore her lucky briefs, red knit ones with a button fly and printed with little blue horseshoes. We both wore dark colors in order to blend into the night; after all, this was a stealth operation. Lucky cursed as she pulled her black turtleneck over her head. "Fuck, it's hot! Maybe we should move the Solstice Gift announcement night to Halloween. At least it'd be cooler."

"We can stop off for ice cream at Herrell's on the way home," I suggested hopefully as I pulled on my black jeans and buttoned up the fly.

We packed our backpack with the Solstice Gift list, a hammer, six thumb tacks, and a bandanna to wipe up any messes. After much grousing about the weather, Lucky and I drove to Thornes Marketplace where Herrell's Ice Cream was located, parked in the nearby garage with the sign that said "Welcome to Northampton. Where the coffee is strong and so are the women…and the first hour in this garage is always free," trudged up the hill to the Smith College campus and on to Paradise Pond, then made our way down the dirt pathway to our oak tree. Someone had left a tiny bouquet of purple pansies wrapped in a white crocheted doily at the foot of the tree. Lucky picked up the sweet little tussy mussy and tucked it into our backpack as I tacked the Solstice Gift list to the tree. We scrambled back up the pathway and strolled back down the hill to the main drag and Herrell's, where I got a cone of apricot bliss ice cream and Lucky got a cone of brown cow.

CHAPTER TWELVE
A Showdown at The Co-Op

Sunday, December 1, 2019

The choosing of the Solstice Gift by Lucky and I always started over breakfast on the first Sunday of December and ended on Pearl Harbor Day, December 7th. I suppose it's possible that it could start at a more civilized hour and over brunch instead of breakfast, but we're old folks and like to wake up early. We usually wake up at 4:00 a.m., then turn to one another all sleepy and cozy under our quilts, fuck our way into the winter morning, and then slowly rise and dress to cook breakfast. Most mornings, breakfast is just plain homemade yogurt mixed with nuts and a pot of black tea or a carafe of coffee, except for Sunday mornings. Sunday mornings are special, and Sunday mornings in December are extraordinarily special because this is when we choose our Solstice Gift. It's like all the treats of your birthday, except every single Sunday of the month. Some Sundays we made overnight yeasted waffles covered with a fruit compote, and other Sundays we made Lucky's specialty, a wild mushroom and goat cheese omelet and toast spread with butter and sweet sticky jam.

On this particular Sunday, December 1st, we broke culinary tradition, and ate both differently and a little later.

The weather had finally cooled down, the leaves had come off the trees, and winter was upon us, so we decided to warm up the house by turning on the oven and baking. I made a creamy spoon bread and fried tart apples, while Lucky whipped up a spinach and goat cheese frittata and Cajun sausages. After breakfast, we fired up the wood stove and drank our coffee in the living room, surrounded by sleeping cats. It had started to snow during the night, but just faintly. Lucky rose from the cushioned depths of her armchair, walked over to the side table, opened the middle drawer, and drew out a well-worn purple moleskin Solstice Gift notebook. Flipping through the pages, she found December 2019, scribbled a few more notes in the notebook, sighed with contentment, and turned the pages back to December 2017. Lucky gazed fondly at the end page for that year, with notes scrawled in green ink and a photo of a beaming Marilyn sandwiched between Lucky and I, the bed sheets and quilts rumpled and our cheeks rosy with postcoital bliss. "Do you remember when we had Marilyn over as the Solstice Gift?" Lucky asked.

I giggled. "Boy, do I ever! I will never drive past the Golden Nozzle Car Wash without thinking about Andrea Dworkin." My cunt got wet and my clit jumped just thinking about that year's threesome.

I tumbled Francy from my lap, got up, and kissed the top of Lucky's greying head. "Now, gather your things; we need to go to the co-op for groceries, and I want to go to that estate sale over on Route 5. I heard that there's a set of Eastlake dining room chairs and someone's grandma's fabric stash from the 1940s."

By the time we were almost ready to leave the house, the snow had picked up and it was snowing fast and hard, that sideways snowfall that I always find so annoying and difficult to watch. It makes me dizzy and cross-eyed. From the kitchen window, we looked at the snow that quickly piled up outside, reminding us, as the lacy white flakes swirled through Sunday morning, "This is it for a while. Bundle up, little traveler!" I watched the winter birds flit about as I wrote out our grocery list for the week: "Bird seed (black-oil sunflower seed, good mixed seeds, and suet), skinless chicken thighs, hard cheddar cheese–white, MORE COFFEE, toilet paper, canned diced tomatoes, those fancy dried chickpeas from California, honey, maple syrup, greens but not fucking kale, one bag of apples, garlic."

Lucky looked down at my list. "I need lemon juice and coconut to make lemon bars," she noted.

"Oooh, lemon bars!" I shimmied in anticipation. "I love your lemon bars, sweetpea!"

"No, silly, it's for work. We're having the monthly birthday potluck, and Artemis begged me to bake my lemon-coconut bars. I can make a little side pan for us though. Okay?"

Lucky went outside to warm up the car, while I bundled up and gathered our grocery bags, then piled into our car with her. The windshield wipers made a soft swooshing noise as they cut through the wet snow. Lucky wore the overstuffed down parka that I gave her for Christmas last year, the striped one that made her look rather majestically like an ocean liner ready to set sail. The jacket was in three shades of blue, with the stripes running diagonally, it was very 1970s disco meets Art Deco moderne. She looked dashing with her round red German cheeks, bright cobalt blue cap, and deep dimples, and I felt my heart melt as we drove through town.

We pulled into the parking lot of the co-op, got out, slid across the parking lot, and made our way into the warm store. That's how it all started, and here we were, five years later, sauntering into the co-op, discussing this year's Solstice Gift. My glasses steamed up and we both stuffed our leather gloves into our pockets. We'd gotten chickpeas, nuts, and flour in the bulk section when it happened. There were three of the prospective Solstice Gifts in the bulk bin section of the co-op, all flirtatiously giving one another the sexy side-eye. Raven was wearing her standard daytime outfit of overalls, a striped T-shirt, combat boots, and a hardhat, Trixie was in a BLM hoodie and red plaid flannel-lined jeans with rolled up cuffs, and Scout was channeling her inner lumberjack with enough plaid flannel and worn denim to clothe a small California mining town.

I giggled at the three of them huddled together. This had happened before and, truthfully, it could go one of two ways; either everyone would get competitive or they would get lascivious. Today, it looked like lascivious was the winner. "Hi Trixie, Raven, and Scout! Small co-op, isn't it!"

"Fancy meeting you all here!" Lucky squeaked. These situations were too reminiscent of awkwardly bumping into exes for Lucky, and it made her nervous.

Trixie blushed, Scout winked, while Raven grinned and flung one arm over Scout's diminutive shoulders and another arm around Trixie's waist. Trixie looked a bit petrified but relaxed under Raven's warm grasp.

See, everyone in the county knew about our Solstice Gift. Hell, every dyke in the surrounding four counties knew about the tradition and knew who the other Solstice Gift contenders were. They all knew, and they had vied with verve and cunning to be picked. After all, we were the Valley's hottest Daddy-Daddy dyke couple. This made being out and about during the winter holiday season… interesting, and often more than a little steamy.

I hugged Trixie, Raven, and Scout tightly, while Lucky shifted from boot to boot, examining her fingernails with embarrassment. "It's so nice running into you all here," I said, to break the ice. We chit chatted about cooking projects; if Swiss chard was better than kale, whether it was truly necessary to salt eggplant to remove the bitterness, how much lemon juice to add to hummus, and the ridiculous number of ingredients needed to make a tasty gluten-free flour baking mixture. After half an hour in the bins, we hugged good-bye. "We'll call you soon," I said.

We skedaddled across the store and away from Trixie, Raven, and Scout. Lucky looked relieved, and I added two chocolate bars to our basket, a dark one with caramel for myself and a milk chocolate one for Lucky.

"I'm partial to Sheila," I exclaimed. "I like to write over at the Pie Bar. When she cuts me a piece of coconut cream pie, glancing at me from under her green bandanna head-wrap with that look of stern flirtation in her light brown eyes, I melt a little. Well, maybe a lot," I sighed in fond remembrance of both the pie and the woman.

"And pie. I mean, you like pie," Lucky said distractedly, and she held the jar a couple feet from her face and squinted at the ingredients list on a jar of fig preserves.

I fished Lucky's reading glasses out of her shirt pocket. "Try these," I told her dryly as I handed her the glasses. "Yes, pies. Sheila brought that delectable blackberry ginger pie Solstice Gift offering two weeks ago. The one with the fancy-pants topping of pastry hearts!"

"Yep. And Raven brought those bitters…" Lucky said.

"What's with naming all the girls in the family after colors?" I interrupted Lucky. "Did you know that Ebony and Raven have a cousin named Indigo, another named Midnight, and a third named Onyx?"

"Ebony told me once that both her mom and her mom's twin sister were underground activists and poets in the civil rights movement, and it isn't just *any* colors, but they are all named for different shades of black," Lucky explained, picking up a package of roasted unshelled pistachios.

I rolled my eyes. "Eh? But that doesn't make any sense at all! Midnight and Indigo are blue, not black!"

"I think the moral of the story is not to mess with the baby name choices of pregnant, underground activist, lesbian poets," Lucky countered. "Anyway, before we got sidetracked, Raven brought over a twelve-pack of herb bitters for making mocktails, the amber bottles wrapped up in colored tissue paper, and Scout serenaded us by playing 'Moon River' on a saw and tossing us chocolates and truffles by the light of the full moon. She was so hot, standing there in her little purple wool suit, red silk bow tie, and red pointy-toed cowboy boots with the snow falling all around, *trés* romantic and suave."

"Well, at any rate, those bitters were adorable! I was especially fond of the fennel and the black current ones. Trixie left bacon and sausage that she's cured herself. I mean, I was impressed that she discovered my weakness for peppered bacon, but I'm a little scared of someone so efficient that she can create an authentic tasting Virginia pork product in just a couple of months!" I shuddered. "I know this sounds silly, but I'd be afraid that she might bring that intensity beyond the bed and want more from us than we're able to give."

Lucky nodded. "Flynn, the librarian, hasn't brought anything over yet. That's odd. I wonder if she knows about the Solstice Gift custom. I mean, I suppose the whole Solstice Gift tradition is a little different. I don't think they do this in Iowa or wherever she moved here from," she added sarcastically.

I rolled my eyes at Lucky as we approached the check-out line. "Don't be snarky. Do you need a snacky-snack, baby?"

Lucky looked contrite and fished around in our groceries for a couple of dried figs. We left the co-op and drove home, quibbling about who to choose for the Solstice Gift, put the groceries put away, and struck out for the estate sale, still discussing the respective merits of Trixie, Raven, Scout, Flynn, and Sheila.

We agreed that although Trixie was brilliant, handsome, and charming, it was far too likely that she might not agree to the limited perimeters of the longest night, so sadly she was out. We adored Ebony's cousin Raven but decided that since we were such close friends with Ebony that fucking Raven was too close for comfort to fucking family. Sheila's elderly mother in Indiana had recently taken a spill, and Sheila needed to fly out for a few weeks until her mom was back on her feet, which meant that my not-so-secret crush was discarded like a soggy piecrust. This left Flynn of the marvelous ass, cataloging abilities, and a brain for miles, and the flirtatious, romantic, and musical Scout.

The snow sped up again as we arrived at the estate sale, and by the time we returned home and parked in front of our home it obscured the front porch. From the back seat of the car, we grabbed the bundle of vintage woolen and cotton fabric and a motley looking fez that we'd gotten at the estate sale and made our way through the flurries to the front door. And there, on the little red table next to our antique twig rocker, were two beautiful large, vintage, barrel-shaped glass jars with brass spigots.

"Oh my, our lovely Flynn came through!" I exclaimed as I brushed the glistening snowflakes off the jar. I peered at the jar's murky contents. "Oh, dear. I believe she has left us sludge!"

Lucky kneeled down on the doormat, her knees creaking, turned on the spigot, ran her forefinger under the dark liquid, then sniffed and licked it. "It's kumbucha, you silly goose! I bet she brewed it herself. What a clever little librarian!"

I shuddered. Kumbucha had never crossed my lips, and it wasn't going to start now if I could help it. I never quite understood the craze for fermentation, although Lucky had been known to pickle anything that moved, so to speak. I tried to hide my trepidation, but a deep sigh gave me away.

Lucky stood up, glaring at me with mock severity. "You *will* drink Flynn's kumbucha, and you *will* appreciate it!"

Lucky did not go Full Daddy on me very often but clearly a line had been drawn concerning etiquette, and if I had any sense at all, I was not going to cross it. I gathered up the glass barrels of kumbucha and brought them inside, their contents sloshing merrily.

Once inside, we warmed up two dishes of left-over winter squash, goat cheese, and hazelnut gratin and ate, then I poured us each a small crystal sherry glass of the dreaded kumbucha, while Lucky lit the wood-burning stove in the living room. If I was going to be forced to drink pickled green tea, I would do it in style. We sat in front of the flame and raised our glasses. "To solstice! May the best woman win!" I toasted and sipped the kumbucha bravely.

Lucky filled her pipe with a honeyed herbal mixture and was settled down in front of the flame. She looked pleased at my efforts at drinking the sludge, then gravely swirled her kumbucha in the glass. "Did you know that kumbucha culture can be dried and made into clothing?" she mused.

"No, I did not know that," I replied tartly. Sometimes Lucky was filled with strange random facts. Much like that jar of kumbucha, you never knew what would come pouring out when you turned on the spigot. "There's hair shirts of course, and a kumbucha shirt sounds the same; an uncomfortable and unappealing garment for penitents and ascetics, except stinky on top of it all! Why would one want a shirt made of fermented green tea?" I grumped.

"If you aren't nice, then I'll give you a kumbucha shirt for the holidays, Mister Bird." Lucky sipped her kumbucha delicately, pinky extended, and head wreathed in wispy smoke from her pipe.

I snorted. "Oy, I can see it now. The next thing you know we'll be printing calling cards with homemade ink that we produce from poke berries and black walnut husks gathered in little baskets as we traipse through the woods like witches."

"Yes!" Lucky cried excitedly, "One of those Victorian black cast iron presses…"

We spent the rest of the evening deep in conversation about calling cards, printing presses, homemade ink, deckled paper, calling card trays, gilding, and proper etiquette for visits. At 10:00 p.m., Lucky yawned and stretched. "Baby, let's go to bed and pick the Solstice Gift."

We toddled upstairs, both the wooden steps and our knees creaking, then cranked up the radiator, undressed, crawled into our chilly bed, and pulled the down comforter and blankets up to our chins.

"Well," Lucky said as she spooned me from behind and nibbled on my shoulder like a squirrel with a particularly delicious sunflower seed, "So, it's between Flynn and Scout. I love Flynn's librarian brain and her juicy ass; however, I also love Scout's playfulness and how her eyes go perfectly round and shiny when she's flirting, like glass marbles."

I squirmed closer to Lucky's warmth. "I have a weakness for catalogers; there's something about assigning call numbers that turns my crank, but Flynn is new to the Valley and I don't know if she's…"

"Ripe?" Lucky interjected, as she tweaked my right nipple.

"Yes, ripe," I moaned. "That's exactly what I mean. I know it doesn't make any sense, but I like our Solstice Gifts to have lived here for at least five years. Scout is a regular Casanova though, and I have mixed feelings about inviting a would-be player into our boudoir, even if she does play the accordion."

"And the saw! Scout is not a player; she's just playful. There is a difference, you know. Remember, you thought I was a player when we first met!" Lucky protested.

"You *were* a player, Mister Otter. You racked up girls like hooligans racked up billiard balls in River City. Hell, you even got your name because of your proclivities for threesomes while you were still a tender butch in college." I felt Lucky shrug her shoulders nonchalantly.

"But I stopped with those shenanigans when I turned 40," Lucky pointed out, as she started snaking her fingers lower and across my soft belly to my cunt.

I pushed back against Lucky's belly, willing her to touch me. I could feel the heat of her body beneath the blankets, warming up us both. I moaned, and my legs parted to welcome her fingers. I loved being under the heavy blankets and comforter with Lucky when it started turning colder at night. The house was still, except for an occasional creak of the wooden floorboards as one of the cats traveled between rooms, and I could see the black night sky scattered with bright stars outside of our bedroom window. The snowstorm had ended, and the sky had cleared. The radiator made a hissing sound, and I could still smell the remains of dinner and Lucky's pipe smoke throughout the house.

My asshole twitched, wanting her cock inside of me, but I was sleepy, maybe too tired for the complicated ritual of choosing accoutrements: a cock, the harness, and lube, and then cleaning up afterward. I chided myself for overthinking things and being a whiny-butt, grateful as always that Lucky couldn't read my mind. God knows, my indecisiveness annoyed myself, so I'm sure that Lucky would be less than enthralled with the verbal sparring that occupied my brain. "Fuck me," I finally managed.

Lucky bounded up from bed, not at all like a bowlful of jelly, and I fetched the wand from the hook on the bedpost. "The long thin one, honey," I requested shyly.

Lucky rummaged in the trunk at the foot of the bed, fit my favorite cock into her harness, pulled it up, and lubed liberally. I was already wet, but I added more lube. I rubbed my clit, teasing it as it became thicker and harder, poking out between my labia.

"Let me see it, baby," Lucky pleaded, her voice husky.

I made my fingers into a V and spread my labia, letting my clit stick out a couple of inches—red, shiny with my pre-come, and swollen, a testament to my lust for Lucky. I jerked off my clit for Lucky, tugging at it slowly, and teased her. Lucky did the same, her hand sliding up and down her cock, her eyes narrowed with desire. As she gripped her cock's head, I begged, "Baby, fuck me. Slide your cock into my ass. I want you all the way in." I turned onto my belly, lifted my ass to Lucky and continued to jerk off. "Do it!"

I could feel the narrow tip of Lucky's cock resting on my asshole and backed up onto it, trying to suck her cock inside of me. There's something to be said for an experienced and determined asshole; my asshole knew what it liked, and it liked to be stuffed. Lucky drew back, and I felt the lubed-up cock slap against my upper thigh. "Aren't you a greedy one, Mister Bird!" Lucky gave me a light whack on my ass, and I whimpered. She started entering me again. "Stay still."

I froze. It wasn't easy though. All I wanted was to fling my asshole violently against Lucky's cock and ride it until we both came with roars. It was torment to feel her enter me inch by inch, but a sweet torment. Finally, Lucky was all the way inside of my ass. She stopped and rested there as if she'd just pulled into the last parking spot in a crowded lot, crowing at having fought off all the other circling drivers and pleased with herself. I wiggled in impatience. As Lucky drew out of my ass slowly, I felt my clit tighten and pulse. She waited a second, the head of her cock rested in my asshole, then drove deep into me. I grunted with surprise; I mean, my brain expected it but it took a minute for my cunt to catch up. Lucky started fucking me. She fucked me just the way I love it, drawing out slowly then slamming down vigorously. We fucked under the covers, the quilt and comforter bulked up over our lumpy forms like the snow on top of mountains, getting steamy inside with the heat of our late night, sleepy fucking. Lucky and I both came quickly: I urged her on to shoot deep inside of my asshole and, with a low groan, Lucky obliged.

I find comfort in sexual regularity the same way I find comfort in a weekday breakfast of yogurt mixed with slightly salted cashews and coffee with cream. I find comfort in using the same vintage cat orgy mug for coffee but the turquoise Fiestaware mug for tea. I find comfort in taking the exact same route when I walk from home to the library. Repetition is my ballast. I love getting fucked the same way by Lucky, day-after-day and week-after-week. I love that when I say, "Deeper. Fill me up. Shoot inside of me!" Lucky comes and then within minutes, I come. I love the tender moments afterward when we cuddle one another to sleep. Our desire (and our exhaustion afterwards) is dependable. And I love the ritual of the Solstice Gift, the way the process starts in early summer, the love-filled purple moleskin book of names, the winnowing of the names by Lucky and me during the hot humid summer months. I love the posting of the final Solstice Gifts on the same exact oak tree near Paradise Pond every autumn equinox and the posting of the final Solstice Gift name on December 7th, the courtship period between December 7th and the winter solstice filled with flirtatious rendezvous and planning with the new Solstice Gift for the longest night, and then our beloved threesome each winter solstice. There was a wondrous regularity in the fact that each Solstice Gift was unique, each longest night a shining star never to be duplicated. And in this, I was comforted.

CHAPTER THIRTEEN
Butter Chicken and a Winner

Monday, December 2, 2019

The next day, Lucky went to work, and I stayed home with Bear and Francy and worked on my memoir. Lucky and I discussed Scout and Flynn over yogurt and coffee during breakfast, then quibbled over the two of them in a flurry of texts during the day. I had agreed with Lucky that fucking Raven was too incestuous and that Trixie was too clingy, and Lucky had vetoed Sheila. I wasn't convinced that Scout wasn't a player, nor was I convinced that Flynn was ready to be the Solstice Gift. I was in that wishy-washy frame of mind that usually causes Lucky to go more than a little apeshit at my acute indecisiveness, but I'm a Libra and that's the way I've always been. I made Indian butter chicken with puffy warm naan and Shirazi salad for dinner that night and set the kitchen table with a Midcentury tablecloth that we'd found at a yard sale that summer. I knew in my heart of hearts that Lucky was right about Scout, so when I brought out a little pottery dish of sticky *gulab jamun* for dessert, I told Lucky that I thought Scout should be the Solstice Gift this year. Lucky lit up with glee, delighted to finally start the process of planning the longest night.

CHAPTER FOURTEEN
Pearl Harbor Day by Paradise Pond

Saturday, December 7th

The night of Saturday, December 7th was auspicious for tramping into the woods by moonlight. It was our favorite kind of early winter night for posting the Solstice Gift winner, lightly snowing, but already with a small accumulation of snow on the ground, yet not too bitterly cold. We parked near Paradise Pond and our oak tree and walked down the hill hand-in-hand in the snow. The sidewalk and the path were slippery and at one point I nearly took a spill but righted myself, laughing. We arrived at the tree, our boot heels crunching in the snow, Lucky dusted the tree trunk off with her red bandana, and I tacked the notice to the tree announcing Scout as the newest Solstice Gift. We made our way back to our car and stopped at Woodstar Cafe for two mugs of hot chocolate and a shared piece of pumpkin cheesecake to celebrate. Lucky didn't discover until we were back in the warmth of our home that she must have dropped her red bandana in the woods, but we figured that someone would enjoy the unexpected gift.

CHAPTER FIFTEEN
Lucky Gives Behrouz a Surprise Holiday Gift

Sunday, December 8th

Lucky and I woke up that morning, giggling. It was always like this during the weeks between Pearl Harbor Day and the longest night, this sense of unbridled anticipation and glee at what lay ahead. Lucky snuggled up to me under the covers as we both listened to the muffled silence of newly fallen snow and the cast iron radiator as it creakily fired up for the morning.

"Hey, baby. I made us a surprise." Lucky hugged me in excitement. "Do you want it now?"

I wiggled my ass against Lucky, but Lucky could hardly contain herself and was already half out of the bed. She threw on her green plaid flannel robe, dashed out of the bedroom, down the hallway and into the studio, and returned holding something behind her back. "Guess what it is!" she proclaimed as she hopped from foot to foot.

My dad used to play this game with me when I was a little girl, and I would always guess the most improbable and outrageous things. "An elephant!" I shouted.

"No. Guess again!"

"A set of hand-carved wooden Eastlake-style tit clamps!"

Lucky cocked her head and raised her eyebrows. "No, but I'm impressed. Guess again."

"Hmmmm...a collection of first edition lesbian trash paperbacks with lurid covers! No, I got it. A ferocious mountain lion. Grrrr!" I collapsed onto the bed pillows laughing and growling with my best mountain lion imitation.

"No, silly." Lucky brought an object out from behind her back. "It's a Solstice Gift Advent calendar!" She bounced back over to the bed and sat down, narrowly missing Francy, who'd taken advantage of Lucky's absence and crawled under the quilt. "Go on, open the door!"

I opened the tiny paper door to December 1st in the Solstice Gift Advent calendar and found a miniature ink drawing of Lucky and I as an otter and a raven. "Aw, it's us as Mister Otter and Mister Bird!" I opened the door to December 2nd to find two chocolate covered espresso beans and popped one into Lucky's mouth, while I ate the other. The door marked December 3rd revealed a tiny stuffed bear and a drawing of the delectable Pooh Bear. December 4th had a bit of sticky honeycomb wrapped in waxed paper with a photo of Honey; December 5th had a tiny silk flower, a penny and a drawing of Penny; December 6th had a dollhouse sized nozzle painted gold and a photo of Marilyn. December 7th had a miniature bottle of blue fingernail polish and a gold framed drawing of Leroy. My hand hesitated over today, December 8th.

I handed the Advent calendar back to Lucky. "Maybe you should open up today, baby."

Lucky passed it back to me. "No, I made it. It's for you to open."

I opened December 8th to reveal a rolled-up piece of parchment tied with a red ribbon, untied the ribbon, and unfurled the paper. It was a menu edged with drawings of pinecones and fir branches and topped with the words "S.S. Solstice" in ornate letters. "It's a ship's menu!" I exclaimed excitedly as I read the menu out loud: "Fruit: Broiled Sugared Grapefruit; Cereal: Semolina; Fish: Kippers; Eggs: Fried Omelet; Hot Cakes: Buckwheat Pancakes; Beverages: Java. Whoa! I'm impressed. Is this today's breakfast? Are you cooking?"

"At your service. Welcome to the S.S. Solstice, where we feed our guests the finest artisanal, gourmet cuisine in western Massachusetts!" Lucky stood and bowed.

I threw off the covers and pulled on my flannel pajama bottoms and a long-sleeved thermal top. Lucky was obviously too keyed up to fuck around in bed this morning, besides we needed to call Scout and make a coffee date to discuss the longest night. We wandered into the kitchen, put the kettle on to boil for coffee, and fed Francy and Bear. After some discussion, Lucky agreed that perhaps the S.S. Solstice menu was a bit overindulgent for today, and we agreed upon a breakfast of broiled grapefruit, cheddar cheese omelets, and coffee. Lucky opened a tin of smoked kippers, much to Francy and Bear's delight, and I stuck to my favorite, peppered bacon.

The weeks between December 8th and December 21st went swiftly. We met with Scout each Wednesday evening for dinner, and discreetly pumped Scout about her desires.; we messaged Scout's best friends, Dylan and April, in our efforts to discover Scout's sexual proclivities; we mailed Scout letters with cunningly cute drawings of critters dressed as Scouts performing filthy deeds; we drank endless cups of tea into the night at Woodstar Cafe. In the end, it appeared that Scout was well-named. Scout was adamant that her sexual passion was to serve.

This posed a conundrum for Lucky and I. We had neatly planned the Solstice Gift as service, our service to the community and to our Solstice Gifts. Scout's passion to serve threw us into a tizzy; what do we do when our Solstice Gift's only desire is to serve us? As Lucky put it one afternoon over gyros and fries at Filo's Greek Tavern: "But who is wurs shod, than the shoemakers wyfe, With shops full of newe shapen shoes all hir lyfe?"

I sprinkled more pepper on my side of the plate of fries and crammed another hot French fry into my mouth. "What the fuck? Speak English."

"The shoemaker and their needs. Scout provides service and never gets sexual service in return. That's it! We can service Scout."

Lucky and I continued our scheming over the final ten days leading up to the solstice. Every morning over coffee, we opened a new paper door to the Solstice Gift Advent calendar, letting loose with a stream of poems, candies, drawings, and miniature toys, and every morning we discussed Scout. One Saturday afternoon, we met with Scout's friends Dylan and April over scones and chai at Woodstar Cafe, where Dylan confided that although Scout could be a masochist, she had a low pain tolerance and a preference for providing sexual service. April added that Scout enjoyed fisting her tops. We knew that it was likely that what Scout loved to give, was also what she secretly yearned to get. We tucked each bit of valuable information away like fat little squirrels storing acorns for the encroaching winter.

The weekend before the longest night we cleaned the house, shopped for groceries and supplies, and planned the dinner menu. Scout had swooned at *fesenjān* (Persian pomegranate, walnut, and chicken stew) when we'd made it for the Orphans dinner, so we prepared *fesenjān*, rice with *tahdig*, and for an all-American wintery dessert, gingerbread with pumpkin ice cream and warm caramel sauce. Scout was a closet old-fashioned romantic, so we wanted to make the house and the bedroom as seductive and relaxing as possible. Green was her favorite color, so we ironed the sage green table linens, tumbled our forest green flannel sheets with a sandalwood scented dryer ball, and arranged a low floral arrangement for the dining room table consisting of red amaryllis, two-tone succulents, evergreen, and white roses. We strung clear fairy lights along the bedroom picture rail and compiled a song list for the night. We bought a couple of sandalwood pillar candles, a bottle of back-up lube and, on a whim, a lovely curved green silicone dildo.

Like Scout, we were prepared.

CHAPTER SIXTEEN
Service is as Service Does

Saturday, December 21ˢᵗ

When Scout knocked on our door at 6:30 p.m. on Saturday, December 21st, she stood shyly in the doorway. Snow clung to her well-worn leather jacket, her rainbow striped scarf was wound twice around her neck, she wore a red knit beanie with an oversized pom-pom on top like a cherry, and her blue spectacles were damp with flakes. We were ready for her, as excited as children on Christmas Eve. As usual, we were both a little nervous, maybe a little more than usual with Scout; after all, it was different when we were seducing the Solstice Gift into something they didn't know that they desperately needed, rather than giving them something that they only wanted.

Sometimes the trajectory of the longest night was clear. Look at Marilyn who was known for being a sadistic top; when the three of us had negotiated with her, she'd finally confessed one late night at 1:00 a.m. that ever since the election, her deepest desire was abject humiliation. She blamed this sudden interest on the egregious awfulness of current politics, but in my opinion, people change all the time. Proclivities evolve and mutate, sometimes for one night and sometimes for longer. On the other hand, Honey wanted to top us together and fill us up like a gas station, so we jumped into her arms like puppies—easy-peasy simple. Like Marilyn, Leroy was used to being in charge. She was a stone top, but we'd had a hunch that Leroy needed two Daddies, so we ran with it, and we were spot on. Providing sexual service was clearly a skill. But Scout, dear Scout...

Scout was puppy-like in her eagerness, all bright-eyed and perky. If she had a tail, she would have been wagging the damn thing. She was a gentleman and brought wine and flowers for the longest night; a bouquet of poppies, pansies, and pine, and a bottle of delicate pink rosé wine. She held the dining room chairs for us, tried to light the candles at the table, and we had to restrain her from actually serving the meal. After we were done eating, we allowed her to clear the table, just so she could work off a little of her nervous energy. We moved into the living room, where Scout lit the wood stove. The three of us settled onto the long velvet sofa, with Scout between us.

With the living room lights dimmed and the flickering woodstove fire lulling us into relaxation, I glanced at Scout and smiled. Scout was still high-strung, waiting for direction. Finally, she cracked. "What do you want? I'm here to service you both! It's what I do."

"Oh baby, don't you worry about that," I purred, and softly kissed Scout on her lips.

Lucky wrapped her arms around Scout and nuzzled her neck, nibbling it tenderly. Scout relaxed as Lucky and I kissed and caressed her, her body finally loosening up beneath our hands. Occasionally, she would remember that she was there to service, and she would panic, but our plan to lull her into a hedonistic stupor was working. I untucked Scout's button-down shirt, and wiggled my hand under it to her sports bra, then found her hard nipples through the cloth and pinched them. Scout moaned into Lucky's ear as I played with her nipples, and Scout tried to find my breasts. I brought her wandering fingers to my mouth and sucked on them, while I unbuckled Scout's wide leather belt.

Lucky whispered, "Come on baby, let's take this into the bedroom," and led Scout into our bedroom, turning on the fairy lights as we walked in the door.

Scout gaped at the sight of the clear sparkling lights circling the bed. "Ooooh, it's so pretty!"

Lucky lit the sandalwood candle on the dresser, while I kissed Scout again and pulled her jeans and briefs down. "It's all for you, baby. It's all for you."

The three of us tumbled into the bed, the velvety flannel sheets cradling us, and made out. Scout was determined to please us; we worked double-duty at distracting her. With four hands caressing her, two mouths kissing and licking her, four legs intertwined with her two legs, and two hot naked bodies pressed up against her, it was a struggle for Scout to maintain her service top equilibrium, but she gave a valiant effort. Finally, I played my secret card—although I didn't know it was my secret card at the time—and tugged at Scout's silvery pompadour. Scout's round eyes rolled up into the back of her head as she gave out a deep moan. I tugged again, delighted at her reaction. Lucky looked up from where she had been kissing Scout's belly and raised her eyebrows. I wiggled my eyebrows back, smiled at Lucky conspiratorially, and pulled on Scout's hair again. As I pulled, Lucky parted Scout's thighs, her hand and mouth inching towards Scout's eager cunt. Scout and I kissed, our mouths open and seeking and Scout's arms wrapped around my neck. I could tell when Lucky had reached Scout's cunt because Scout's body melted in my arms, then she started moaning into my mouth. Finally, she broke loose from our kiss, words spilling from her lips: "Fuck, fuck, fuck. Oh, god, yes!" and I felt Scout's body stiffen and shake as she came.

After that first orgasm, Scout panicked, worried that we were disappointed in her, that she had let us down by not serving us. Lucky and I petted her, stroking her head and kissing her shoulders and neck softly. We reassured her that she was perfect in every way and exactly what we wanted. The three of us took a chocolate break, feeding one another caramels in bed until everyone was calm again, then slowly resumed making out. The longest night was a tangle of Scout coming, slippery cunts, sweaty bodies, and moans, the bedroom filled with the musky scent of come and pheromones. At 1:00 a.m., Scout and I were stuck together like dogs in heat, my pink nipples pressed into her hard brown nipples, while Lucky filled Scout's luscious open cunt, first with one finger, then two, three, four, and finally slipping her entire hand into her cunt as Scout thrashed and shouted into the night, "More, more! Deeper, please! Fuck me!" While Lucky fisted Scout, I rubbed my soaking wet cunt against Scout's hip, pressing my clit hard against the hipbone and imagining my foreskin sliding up and down over my clit's head, until I anointed her with my come. Scout smelled amazing, all dank heat and the smell of fucking rising through her pores, her skin hot and salty.

At 2:00 a.m., the three of us were taking another chocolate and water break, while Francy and Bear had tentatively ventured back into the bedroom, glancing at us sideways as they slunk around the bed as if to double dog dare us into starting our loud shenanigans and wrestling again. We cuddled for a while deep into the night, with Scout playing Lucky Pierre and nestled in-between Lucky and I, just holding onto one another in the still of the moment, until Lucky's hand wandered again, finally flipping Scout onto her tummy like a pancake with me beneath Scout, and Lucky sitting on top, riding Scout's ass like a cowboy. I felt a little breathless laying there buried under Scout and Lucky, but with the delight of both of them coming on top of me, it felt churlish to complain. By 3:00 a.m., Lucky was giving Scout head in a 69 position, while I kneeled on the bed and fucked Scout's ass with the green dildo that we'd bought for the occasion. Fortunately, Scout had long ago given up on being the service top of our dreams. Scout radiated pleasure, and Lucky and I were the eager conduits for Scout's lust. The fairy lights twinkled above like moonshine, illuminating the three of our bodies, and the sandalwood candle filled the air with its spicy scent. By 4:00 a.m., we started to feel our age, sleepy and with knees creaking. I yawned and Scout rubbed her eyes. We finally gave up, our restless hands, lips, and limbs stilled and fell asleep together, a sweaty pile of contented and satiated queers.

The next morning, we had the official bestowment of the order of the *Equestris Dignitas ad Solstitium Donum* to Scout at the breakfast table. We were all giggly and still tired, three sated butches wrapped in plaid flannel robes. Scout was adorable, with her sex-tousled hair, never-ending grin, and her freckled shoulders peeking out of the blue and grey plaid robe. The robe matched the cobalt blue color of her spectacles perfectly. It could have been a postcard for "butch love." Lucky and I assured Scout that she was the best service top ever, because even though it was difficult for her, she'd done exactly what we'd asked her to do, which was to bottom thoroughly. Scout was enchanting as she beamed and teared up with pleasure and embarrassment at the praise, sitting at the breakfast table, the snow falling quietly through Sunday morning outside. I refreshed our cups with more coffee, and we toasted to one another with what had become our ritual—a new year, new pleasures, and new family—"To each and every year's Solstice Gift! Long may we all reign!"

THE END

RECIPE

Khoresh-i Ghormeh Sabzi (fried herb stew)

Khoresh is a popular Persian stew consisting of meat and vegetables or fruit. *Ghormeh* means fried and *sabzi* is herbs. *Khoresh-i ghormeh sabzi* is homey Persian comfort food at its best, a fragrant sweet-sour herb stew served over steamed long-grained basmati rice. Although *khoresh-i ghormeh sabzi* is traditionally made with meat, you can omit it and it's still tasty. *Limoo* and *adveih* can be found at Middle Eastern markets and even through Amazon. Sadaf is a popular Persian foodstuffs brand and their *adveih* is called 7-spice seasoning. *Limoo* are not to be confused with salted preserved lemons. *Limoo* are hard, dark brown, shriveled nuggets of lime intensity!

Ingredients:

Meat:

2 pounds chicken, lamb or beef, washed and cubed

1/2 cup oil

3/4 cup dried red kidney beans, soaked overnight in water

2 large yellow onions, halved and sliced thinly

4 dried limes (*limoo amani*), pierced several times with a knife

Herbs:

4 cups fresh flat-leafed parsley leaves, finely chopped

1 cup fresh cilantro leaves, finely chopped

2 large leeks, green ends and roots removed, chopped and washed thoroughly

1 cup fresh fenugreek, finely chopped, or 3 tablespoons dried fenugreek

Seasonings:

1 teaspoon turmeric (optional)

1 teaspoon *adveih khoresh* (a *khoresh* spice mixture)

2 tablespoons *limoo* powder or 4 tablespoons fresh lime juice

1 teaspoon salt

1/2 teaspoon freshly-ground pepper

Water

Directions:

In a large stew pot, sauté the sliced onions and the meat in 3 tablespoons of oil until browned.

Add salt and pepper.

Clean, wash, and dry the herbs, then chop finely.

Heat 1/3 cup of vegetable oil in a large skillet over medium heat and sauté the chopped fresh herbs and the chopped leeks for 20 to 25 minutes, stirring often. Do not stint on this step! Set aside.

Add the soaked dried beans, fried herbs and the pierced *limoo* to the meat and onions.

Pour in enough water to cover the *khoresh* by about 2 inches, bring to a boil on high, lower the heat, cover, and cook on medium to low heat for 1 1/2 hours.

Add a little more water if needed. Reduce the heat to its lowest setting and simmer for 30 minutes. The longer *ghormeh sabzi* simmers the tastier it becomes!

Serve over steamed basmati rice.

AVERY CASSELL

Avery Cassell is a writer and artist whose books include *Masculinities: boi • bulldagger • butch • masc • MOC • soft butch • stud • tomboy • transmasc* (2023, Stoic Press), 31st Lambda finalist *Resistance: The LGBT Fight Against Fascism in WWII* (2018, Stacked Deck Press), the *Butch Lesbians of the 20s, 30s, and 40s Coloring Book* and the *Butch Lesbians of the 50s, 60s, and 70s Coloring Book*; the erotic romance *Behrouz Gets Lucky* (2016, Cleis Press); and short stories in several anthologies, including *Best Lesbian Erotica 2015*, *Unspeakably Erotic: Lesbian Kink*, *Sex Still Spoken Here*, and *Best Lesbian Erotica of the Year, Volume Four* and *Volume Seven*. Many of their titles can be bought at stoicpress.bigcartel.com, or their Etsy shop, Whippersnapped.

Made in the USA
Middletown, DE
06 April 2024